HEARTLAND™

After the Storm

Read all the books about Heartland:

After the Storm

Lauren Brooke

■ SCHOLASTIC

Picture of DJ courtesy of Vauxhall City Farm.
For more information visit www.vauxhallcityfarm.org

Scholastic Children's Books
An imprint of Scholastic Ltd
Euston House, 24 Eversholt Street
London, NW1 1DB, UK
Registered office: Westfield Road, Southam, Warwickshire, CV47 0RA
SCHOLASTIC and associated logos are trademarks and
or registered trademarks of Scholastic Inc.
Series created by Working Partners

First published in the UK by Scholastic Ltd, 2000
This edition published 2009

ISBN 978 1407 11160 5

British Library Cataloguing-in-Publication Data
A CIP catalogue record for this book is available from the British Library

Printed and bound by CPI Group (UK) Ltd, Croydon, CR0 4YY
Papers used by Scholastic Children's Books are made from wood grown in
sustainable forests.

3 5 7 9 10 8 6 4

www.scholastic.co.uk/zone

Chapter One

Amy tried to scream as she saw her mom open the driver's door to the pick-up. But no words would come out. She wanted to stop her but she couldn't move. She could only watch, horrified, as her mother put the key in the ignition and started the engine.

And then the dream changed.

Now they were both in the pick-up. And the trailer behind them shook as the bay stallion kicked out in fear. Amy tried hard to wake herself up but the dream tightened its hold on her. She was trapped in the same nightmare she had been having over and over again.

Marion's hands gripped the steering wheel tightly. "This is insane," she muttered, her blue eyes looking into Amy's. "I should never have let you talk me into this, Amy."

"Mom!" Amy sobbed desperately. "Stop, please stop." But Marion didn't hear her.

A flash of lightning split the dark sky, and the clattering of hooves in the trailer was drowned out by a huge crash of thunder overhead.

Amy started to scream as tall swaying trees loomed up on the road ahead. Branches closed over the top of the pick-up, banging and scraping along the roof of the trailer. A long, drawn out creak of straining wood was followed by a clap of thunder so loud that it sounded as if a cannon had gone off. Straight in front of them, a tree started to fall slowly into the road...

"*No!*" Amy screamed. "*Please, no!*"

"Amy! Amy! Wake up!"

Amy suddenly felt her shoulder being shaken. She opened her eyes. She was lying on a hard wooden floor. Her grandfather was bending over her, his forehead creased in concern.

"Grandpa," Amy said, sitting up in confusion.

She breathed in a faint, familiar smell of perfume. Photographs of horses stared down at her from the walls. She was in her mother's room. A coat was slung over a chair just where Mom had left it the day of the accident. The hairbrush on the dressing-table was coated in a fine layer of dust, a few blonde hairs caught in the bristles. Nothing in the room had changed for six weeks, not since the night of the storm when Marion Fleming had died.

At the sight of all the familiar things Amy felt her stomach twist. "What am I doing in here?"

Jack Bartlett saw the shock on her face. "It's OK, honey," he said quickly. "You must have been sleep-walking."

"It was a horrible dream," Amy stammered, getting to her feet. The air in the room felt still and quiet. Sweat prickled through her long light-brown hair as she looked around.

"Come on, it's over now," Grandpa said soothingly. "Let's get you back to your own room." He put his arm round her shoulders.

Just then her mom's bedroom door opened. Lou, Amy's older sister, stood in the doorway. "What's happening?" she asked, her short fair hair tousled from sleep. "I heard screaming."

"It's OK," Jack Bartlett said quickly as he steered Amy towards the door. "Amy had a nightmare and was sleep-walking."

"Oh, Amy," Lou said, moving swiftly to Amy's side.

"I'm OK," Amy said, pulling away from Grandpa and pushing past Lou to the door. She just wanted to get out of the room. It was too much to bear, knowing that Mom was never going to come back.

The sheets on her bed felt cool. She pulled them over her. Grandpa and Lou came to the doorway and she saw Grandpa say something to Lou in a low voice.

Lou nodded. "See you in the morning," she said softly to Amy and left.

Grandpa came over and sat on the edge of Amy's bed.

"I'm OK, Grandpa," Amy told him. "You go to bed now, too."

"I'll stay for a bit," Grandpa said.

Amy felt too exhausted to argue. She lay back against the pillows. As her eyes shut, the nightmare flickered around the edges of her consciousness. She blinked.

"Oh, Grandpa," she said, opening her eyes quickly.

"Don't worry, I'm here," Grandpa said gently. He stroked her hair. "Go to sleep now, honey."

When Amy woke in the morning, Grandpa had gone. As always the first thought that flashed into her mind was the hot, quick hope that the last six weeks had never happened. But as she saw the pale morning light filtering through her curtains, reality hit her with an icy certainty – Mom was dead, and it was her fault.

Amy sat up, wrapping her arms around her knees. If she hadn't been so desperate to rescue Spartan, the bay stallion, from the outbuilding where he'd been abandoned by thieves, then Mom would never have gone out in that storm and the accident would never have happened. She had pleaded with her mom to go. A sickening feeling of guilt gripped her heart.

Getting out of bed, Amy pulled on a pair of jeans and went to open the curtains. From her window she could see Heartland's front stable block and the patchwork of turn-out paddocks filled with horses grazing and dozing in the quiet of the early morning sun. Stepping over the clutter of clothes and magazines on her floor, Amy hurried downstairs. She would go and start on the yard chores. She didn't want to think about Mom — just as she didn't want to think about what the day ahead held for her.

Later that afternoon, Amy stood in one of the stalls in the front block and shook out a flake of straw on to the thick, fresh bed. Dust particles floated and danced in the shafts of warm sunlight that shone in over the half-door. She thought about Spartan. Tomorrow he would be standing exactly where she was now. For a moment she almost wanted to be sick. Life felt so unfair.

"Have you finished?" Ty, Heartland's seventeen-year-old stable-hand, looked over the door. He must have read the worry on her face because his eyebrows suddenly furrowed in concern. "Amy? Are you OK?" he asked, walking in.

Amy nodded, not trusting herself to speak.

"Hey," Ty said softly. He looked round the stall. "Are you thinking about Spartan?" Amy nodded again. "It'll be fine," he said, squeezing her arm sympathetically. "You'll see."

From down the yard came the sound of the farmhouse door opening. "Amy! Ty!" Jack Bartlett called. "It's almost time to go."

Amy went to the door. "Coming!"

"I'd better get cleaned up," Ty said. "Look, I'll see you down at the house in a minute." Leaving the stall he hurried up the yard.

As Amy shut the half-door she glanced round the stall one more time. The very next day the bay horse would be there.

He would look over his door, waiting to be fed, to be groomed, to be cared for, just like any of the other horses at Heartland. Amy shivered. Who was she kidding? Spartan could never be just another horse to her.

She walked slowly towards the whitewashed farmhouse and let herself in through the back door. Grandpa and Lou were talking quietly in the kitchen. They were both dressed in dark clothes. On the table lay a big bunch of white lilies tied with a black ribbon. They filled the air with a sweet, heavy scent.

"We have to leave soon," Jack Bartlett said. "We said we'd meet Scott and Matt at five-thirty."

Amy nodded. "I'll just change out of my yard clothes," she said, heading for the staircase.

Reaching her bedroom, Amy grabbed a brush and ran it quickly through her hair before twisting it up on top of her head with a slide. Leaving her jeans and T-shirt in a heap, she pulled on a long, black sleeveless dress. She checked her reflection in the dressing-table mirror. Her grey eyes looked large in her pale face.

Her gaze fell on the framed photograph of her mom that she kept by the mirror. She picked it up. It was one of her favourite pictures. Mom, standing by a field gate, laughing as she stroked Pegasus. It had been taken just a few weeks before the accident. Amy felt a stab of pain in her chest.

"Amy!" She heard Lou calling up the stairs.

Putting the photograph down, Amy picked up a piece of

paper from her desk, folded it quickly and put it in her pocket.

Lou was standing at the bottom of the staircase, her normally composed face showing signs of tension. "Ready?" she asked, in her clipped accent, the product of the English boarding school she had attended.

Amy fiddled with the piece of paper in her pocket. "Yeah, I'm ready."

They went through to the kitchen.

Ty was by the door. His long, dark hair was smoothed back and he had put on a clean white shirt and black trousers. His eyes met Amy's with a look of concern. She managed a faint smile in return.

Jack Bartlett opened the back door. "Well, let's go then."

They drove to the cemetery in silence. Scott Trewin, the local equine vet, and his younger brother, Matt, were waiting in the parking lot when they arrived.

"Hey there," Matt said quietly as Amy got out of the car.

Matt and Amy went to the same school and were good friends. In the past, Matt had often intimated that he was interested in them becoming more than that, but today his face showed nothing but friendly concern and sympathy. He smiled warmly. "How are you doing?"

Amy nodded. "Not so bad."

Walking across the memorial ground, Amy thought about the service. Mom's headstone had been laid that morning and Amy wanted to take the opportunity to say a proper goodbye. The official funeral had been held a few days after the accident, six weeks ago, while Amy was still lying unconscious in hospital.

The party reached the shady corner where Marion's headstone was placed. To the left was an older headstone, weathered by the years but with the plot carefully tended around it. Amy saw her grandpa's gaze fall on it, then he walked over and gently touched it, closing his eyes.

It was the grave of Jack Bartlett's wife, the grandmother who had died even before Lou, who was twenty-three, had been born.

After a moment, Grandpa returned to the small group. He cleared his throat. "Well, thanks for coming. As you all know we are here today to say a final goodbye to Marion." He looked round at everyone. "A daughter, a mother – a friend. Each of us has our own special memories of her. She made us laugh, she dried our tears, she listened, she helped, she loved. She cared passionately for all the horses that she took in and healed at Heartland. Marion's love was boundless and I am so proud that she was my daughter."

As Grandpa spoke, Amy focused on the light-grey headstone, the soil around its base still fresh and slightly damp, flowers heaped on the grave. It felt as though Grandpa's words were washing over her, not registering. She stared dry-eyed at the inscription on the stone and read her mom's name, the year she was born and the year of her death, over and over again. She, Lou and Grandpa had chosen the inscription together. It read:

Her spirit will live on at Heartland for ever.

"Amy," Grandpa said softly, breaking through her thoughts. "Will you read the poem you have chosen to remember your mom?"

Amy walked forward and knelt down to lay the lilies at the bottom of the headstone. Then she took her place again beside Lou, who squeezed her hand, tears welling in her eyes. Amy took the folded piece of paper from her pocket and opened it up.

"Mom loved this poem," she said quietly. "She had it pinned to the mirror in her bedroom. Daddy gave it to her when her first horse died. It's called 'The Life That I Have' and it's by Leo Marks." Looking down at the creased piece of paper she started to read:

> "The life that I have
> Is all that I have
> And the life that I have
> Is yours."

As Amy read she noticed that Lou was fighting to stay composed and her grandpa was brushing a hand across his eyes. Amy waited for her own tears to overwhelm her, but none came. She read on, her voice clear, her mind numb.

"The love that I have
Of the life that I have
Is yours and yours and yours.
A sleep I shall have
A rest I shall have
Yet death will be but a pause.
For the peace of my years,
In the long green grass
Will be yours and yours and yours."

There was an audible sob from Lou. Feelings of desperation welled up in Amy. Why wasn't she feeling anything? Why wasn't she crying? Having finished the poem, she walked slowly forward to the grave. "Goodbye, Mom," she whispered, touching the headstone. "Heartland will keep going. I promise."

Grandpa walked up behind her and put his hand on her shoulder. She turned and he kissed her on the forehead. They stood silent for a moment.

As the little group moved slowly back to the car park, each wrapped in their own thoughts and memories, Ty walked alongside Amy. "You OK?" he asked, his eyes scanning her face.

Amy knew that he must be surprised by her lack of tears — it just wasn't in her nature to try and keep her feelings to herself. And yet it wasn't a conscious decision. She wanted to cry, she really did, but something was stopping her. "I'm fine," she replied. She smiled gratefully. "Thanks for coming, Ty."

"I wouldn't have missed it." Ty shook his head, his eyes dark and intense. "Your mom made me believe that I could make it with horses. And I dropped out of school because I knew that I could learn so much more from her – important things that school could never teach me..." His voice echoed his confusion and loss. "I just can't believe she's gone."

Amy touched his arm. Quickly, he covered her hand with his own.

"Amy." Amy jumped and turned. Scott came up to her. "That poem was incredible," he said, looking down at her. "I can see why it meant so much to Marion."

"I know," Amy said. He looked her full in the face and impulsively she changed the subject so that he wouldn't notice her lack of tears. "How ... how's Spartan?" As the name left her lips her stomach tightened. *Spartan*. Scott had chosen the name.

"He's very unsettled," Scott replied. "Physically he's on the mend but mentally he's still traumatized. He's very nervous and wary of people. The accident affected him badly."

Guilt flooded through Amy.

Scott looked at her reassuringly. "But you'll be able to cope with him, Amy," he said. "If anyone can, you can."

* * *

At three o'clock the next day, Amy waited for Scott to arrive with Spartan. Lou and Grandpa were out doing the grocery shopping and it was Ty's day off, so Matt had come round to keep her company.

He kicked a stone down the drive. "Scott should get here soon," he said, glancing at his watch. "He said he'd be here just before three."

"Yeah," Amy replied. Her heart was beating fast at the thought of seeing Spartan again. She was glad that Matt was there. He wasn't into horses in a big way and he didn't fully understand how she was feeling, but just having him around made her feel better.

"Heard from Soraya lately?" Matt asked.

"I got a letter last week," Amy said. Soraya Martin was her best friend. She was away at a summer riding camp and Amy was finding it really tough not being able to speak to her on a regular basis. "She sounds like she's having fun."

"When's she back?"

"Three weeks," Amy replied. "I can't wait." She glanced at her watch nervously. Where was Scott? What was keeping him? He should have been there by now.

She walked over to the big grey horse in the end stall and stroked his nose. He nuzzled her affectionately. She smiled faintly. No matter how she was feeling, Pegasus always seemed to understand. He had been her father's horse – one of the finest showjumpers in the world. But an accident in London twelve years ago had left Daddy too badly injured to ever ride again and Pegasus physically and emotionally damaged.

Amy kissed Pegasus's soft muzzle. It was through nursing Pegasus back to health that Mom had learnt all about the alternative therapies that had inspired her to start Heartland – a horse sanctuary – after her marriage to Tim Fleming had broken down.

Matt came to join Amy. "It's twenty minutes past," he said in concern, looking at his watch. "I hope nothing's happened."

As Amy pulled away from Pegasus, her ears caught the faint chug of an engine coming up the drive. "This is probably him now," she said quickly.

A few seconds later, Scott's battered pick-up came round the corner, a trailer swaying behind it. As it got closer, the sound of hooves thudding against metal could be heard. Matt and Amy exchanged nervous looks.

The pick-up stopped beside them. Scott cut the engine and jumped out. "What a journey!" he said. His face was strained as he nodded to the trailer. "I thought Spartan was going to come out of the back at one point. He hasn't stopped kicking the whole way here."

There was a moment's silence and then a high, whinnying scream rang out, full of rage and fury. Amy jumped as a hoof banged into the metal wall right next to her.

"Wow!" said Matt. "He sounds really mad!"

"He is." Scott looked at Amy. "We'd better get him out. I'll go in and hold him while you two put the front ramp down."

He disappeared in through the side door. There was another series of thuds and the trailer shook.

Amy's heart pounded in her chest as she moved round to unbolt the ramp. Any minute now Spartan would emerge. She remembered him as he had been the night she and her mom had collected him – beautiful and serene. And amazingly friendly considering he was a stallion and had been locked in a dark barn. He wasn't a stallion any more. Scott had gelded him once it looked like he was going to recover and would be coming to Heartland to be rehabilitated and then re-homed.

"Let's go!" Scott called out.

Amy and Matt let down the ramp, jumping aside just in time as Spartan plunged forward with a screaming whinny.

"Easy now! Easy!" Scott shouted.

With a plunge, the horse clattered down the ramp. He stopped still and looked round at the fields and the fences – his bay coat gleaming with sweat, his eyes burning with fire.

Amy stood, frozen. Spartan was unrecognizable. The trust and confidence that was in his eyes the first time she'd seen him had been replaced by fury and fear. Ugly scars stood out along his back and quarters. Once again, guilt flooded through her as she looked at him. She felt a sudden desperate urge to turn and run away – far away.

Suddenly Spartan's head whipped round as he caught her scent. With a squeal of pure rage he lunged towards her, his mouth open, his ears flat against his head. Amy leapt back.

Scott struggled with the halter to get the horse under control. "Are you all right?" he called anxiously to Amy.

"I'm fine," she replied breathlessly.

"We'd better get him into his stall," Scott said.

"I'll get the door," Matt said, edging rather cautiously past Spartan and then hurrying up the yard.

Scott led Spartan after him. The horse jogged and shook his head. He didn't seem to want to take his eyes off Amy, but Scott's voice and his hand on the halter urged him onward.

Scott took him into the stall and secured the door behind him. "Sorry about back there," he said to Amy. "I don't know what came over him. He's been difficult to handle but he hasn't gone for anyone like that before."

"I guess it was probably just the shock of travelling in the trailer," Amy reasoned. "It must have reminded him of the accident." She went to the door and looked over. She noticed Spartan stiffen as he saw her and then, without warning, he plunged at the door, his snapping teeth missing her arm by inches.

"Whoa!" Scott shouted at the horse. Spartan shot to the back of his box again.

"What made him do that?" Matt said to Amy.

She looked quickly at Scott. "He hates me, doesn't he? He knows that it's because of me he was in the accident."

"Not *hates*," Scott said quickly. "Horses don't hold grudges. You know that. But he will associate you with the accident. He's probably attacking you because he's scared — scared that if he lets you get near you'll put him through something similar again."

"So what can Amy do, Scott?" Matt asked, his voice full of concern.

"Rebuild his trust," Scott answered. His eyes met Amy's. "It's going to be a long, slow process — but you've done it before."

Yes, Amy suddenly wanted to shout, *but not without Mom and never with a horse that was scared of me.*

Scott must have seen the doubt on her face. "You can do it, Amy — maybe you're the *only* person who can. If Spartan can come to trust and accept you then he'll be able to trust anyone."

Amy swallowed. She would have to see Spartan every day, face his angry eyes, meet his resentment. She didn't know if she was up to it.

Scott studied her. "Look, if you really don't want to then don't worry," he said. "I'll try and find somewhere else to take him."

Although Scott was hiding his disappointment, Amy knew that it would be a difficult task to find someone else who would help Spartan. She swallowed. "No, I'll do it," she said.

Scott smiled. "Great!" he said, squeezing her shoulder. "And don't worry about it. I know you can do it."

Amy glanced at Spartan's door, wishing she felt so sure.

Chapter Two

Leaving Spartan to calm down, Scott asked if he could take a look at Sugarfoot.

"Sure," Amy said. Sugarfoot was a Shetland pony that she had been nursing back to health.

As they walked up the yard past the turn-out paddocks, Amy stopped to pat a handsome buckskin pony who was looking over the fence. "Hi there," she said. Sundance snorted in reply and thrust his head affectionately into her chest.

"He's looking good," Scott said.

"Yeah," Amy nodded. She fed Sundance a couple of mints.

Too unpredictable and ill-tempered to be re-homed, Sundance was one of the few permanent equine residents at Heartland. Badly behaved with everyone else, he utterly adored Amy and whenever there was time, she took him hunter-jumping in local shows.

"So how's Sugarfoot been?" Scott asked, as they walked on and entered the twelve-stall barn at the top of the yard.

"He's getting much better," Amy said. "He's eating well now."

Sugarfoot had been left in his stable with no food for three weeks after his old owner, Mrs Bell, had died. He'd first arrived at Heartland grief-stricken and had refused to eat, eventually becoming very ill with broncho-pneumonia. He had been so sick that they'd thought they were going to lose him – until a week ago, when he'd turned a corner and started to recover.

Sugarfoot was standing by his hay net. He gave a low, welcoming nicker and walked over to say hello.

"He's looking great," Scott said, stroking the Shetland's thick flaxen mane. "What remedies have you been using?"

Amy ran through the details of the herbs and aroma-therapy oils she had been treating Sugarfoot with. "Diluted neroli oil for massage, then garlic, fenugreek seed and nettles in his feed," she said. "They seem to be working."

"More than just working!" Scott said approvingly. He checked Sugarfoot's breathing and heart rate. "He's improving fast."

"Well, it's Lou really who's been looking after him," Amy explained.

"Lou?" Scott echoed.

It had been a surprise to Amy as well. Ever since their father's accident and the subsequent break-up of their parents' marriage, Lou had refused to have anything to do with horses. Even when she had come to Heartland after their mom's death she had avoided any contact with them. However, the little Shetland had captured her heart and she'd been moved to helping him.

"She spends as much time as she can with him," Amy said.

"How long is she planning on staying?" Matt asked.

"Well, she's told her work that she won't be back until the autumn," Amy said. She patted Sugarfoot gratefully. If it hadn't been for him then Lou would *already* have gone back to her high-powered banking job in Manhattan.

"And what will you do when she does go back?" Scott asked.

Amy shrugged. She didn't want to think about it. When the winter came and she was at school they would just have to find the money to take on another stable-hand — either that or reduce the number of horses. "Maybe she'll change her mind," she said optimistically.

"You think there's a chance?" Scott said in surprise. "I thought she was really into city life."

"She is," Amy admitted. Lou *was* into her job in a big way — her job, her apartment and Carl, her boyfriend. "But she seems to be liking it here. I don't know ... she *might* stay."

Just then there was the sound of a car pulling up outside the house. "That's probably Lou and Grandpa now," Amy said.

They went down the yard. Jack Bartlett's station wagon was parked outside the house and he and Lou were getting out.

"Hi!" Amy called.

"Hi there," Grandpa replied. "Spartan's here, is he?"

"Yes. In the stall at the end," Amy said.

Grandpa and Lou walked curiously over. Amy glanced at Matt, who was drinking a Coke by the back door, and then hurried after them. "Don't go too close," she warned.

Grandpa stopped. "Why?" A look of concern flickered in his eyes as he studied her face. "He's not *dangerous*, is he?"

"No, no, of course not," Amy said quickly. "He's just a bit upset after the journey."

"Well, he's a good-looking horse," Grandpa commented, looking over the door. "A Morgan by the looks of him."

Scott turned to Amy. "Look, I'd better be going now. Ring me if you want any advice, otherwise I'll drop by in a few days." He smiled at her. "Oh, and good luck." He turned to Matt. "Do you want a lift?"

"Yeah, sure," Matt nodded.

They said their goodbyes and then walked down to Scott's pick-up. The engine coughed into life, and then with a belch of exhaust fumes the pick-up and trailer trundled away.

That night, Amy sat up in bed reading until late. She didn't want to fall asleep for fear of facing a nightmare again. Forcing her eyes to stay open she read and read, but as the night wore on the print started to blur and at last her eyes closed.

She was in the dark. But where? Four wooden walls pressed in on her. It was some sort of barn. Rain drummed down on to the tin roof above and the wind howled outside.

Amy wasn't sure why she was in this dark, enclosed space but she had an unrelenting desire to escape. Uneasily, she moved towards the door. There was a sudden crash of thunder followed by a creak as the door slowly opened.

"Mom!" Amy gasped, seeing Marion standing there with her hair plastered to her head and a halter in her hand.

"Easy," Marion soothed. She turned to someone behind her. "Stand back a bit now," she said, putting a hand in her pocket and taking out a tin.

With the next fork of lightning the two silhouettes were lit up and Amy recognized her own figure hovering behind her mom. Suddenly, she realized what was happening – she was seeing the events of the night of the accident through Spartan's eyes, experiencing his fear and bewilderment!

Her mom stepped towards her, offering her hand. There was a clap of thunder, a moment of total blackness and then the scene changed. Amy heard a metal clang as a door shut fast behind her, echoing ominously like a prison door. She realized she was now inside the trailer. She could hear the engine of the pick-up starting and felt the trailer rock as it began to move.

Panic gripped Amy. She knew what was coming next. "Let me out!" she screamed. She lashed out at the metal walls, rocking the trailer, but to no avail. She was trapped. The rain hammered relentlessly against the roof – there was the sound of creaking branches and then she heard it. The spine-chilling, cannon-loud crack of a tree trunk breaking, the sound of squealing brakes, a bang, and then nothing.

* * *

Amy opened her eyes and snapped her light on. Her room seemed eerily quiet. Taking lungfuls of air, her breathing gradually steadied. Reaching out for a book she opened it with shaking fingers. It was still dark outside but she couldn't face going back to sleep.

The minutes crawled by until it was an acceptable time to get up. Amy met Lou down in the kitchen and after grabbing a coffee and a muffin they went outside to feed the horses. The sky was a cloudless blue and the early-morning air was clear and cool.

"What a beautiful day!" Lou said. "You know, on mornings like this it makes Manhattan seem totally unreal. I can't imagine getting up and going to work in the office."

The peace was then shattered as Spartan put his head over his door and upon seeing Amy let out a piercing whistle. He half reared in his stall.

Lou gasped in alarm. "What's the matter with him?"

"It's me," Amy admitted. "He's scared of me because of the accident." She ran a hand through her hair. "Look, it might be best if you feed him. Or we could wait till Ty gets here."

"I'll do it," Lou said. "There's no point waiting for Ty."

They reached the feed-room. "I wonder what Carl will think of it here," Lou said, unscrewing the lid of the cod-liver oil tin as Amy started adding heaped scoops of grain to the buckets. "He's coming in a couple of days."

Amy had only met Carl once when she had been staying with Lou in Manhattan. He hadn't seemed at all interested in hearing about Heartland and Amy had reservations about him.

"I can't imagine it," Lou mused. "I've never been with him in the country." She started to stack up the feeds. "Still, maybe he'll have some ideas for helping this place make money."

"Make money?" Amy echoed.

"Yes," Lou replied, obviously seeing the doubt on Amy's face. "Well, we're going to have to raise some more money somehow — even *you* can appreciate that, Amy. Without Mom it's going to be a struggle to persuade customers to bring their horses here. I know Nick Halliwell said he would bring us some business..."

"And he has," Amy interrupted.

Nick Halliwell was a famous show-jumper who had recently brought one of his best horses to Heartland to have its fear of loading into a trailer cured. It had been the first problem horse that Amy had attempted to heal without her mom. Within two days the horse was going in and out of the trailer with no problem. Nick Halliwell had been very impressed and had promised to recommend Heartland to all his friends. Already two new horses, Raisin and Topper, had arrived to be treated.

"But we can't *rely* on him," Lou pointed out. "We have to try and raise our profile in other ways. I've had some ideas that I'm going to work on this afternoon. I know she did her best, but Mom really didn't run this place in the most economical way. We simply *have* to become more profitable."

She picked up the buckets for the front stables. "It may mean a few changes but I'm sure we can manage."

Amy headed up to the back barn with the other pile of buckets. *A few changes.* She bit her lip. She didn't want changes. She wanted everything to stay just the way it had been before Mom died.

Ty arrived at seven-thirty. He and Amy got stuck into their normal morning routine – turning out horses, cleaning stalls, filling water buckets. As Amy worked she became aware of Spartan watching her. She didn't want to look at him and yet her gaze seemed irresistibly drawn to his stall. Time after time she would glance over and see the hatred in his eyes. On each occasion that she walked anywhere near his stall, his ears flattened and he snapped at the air.

She saw Ty coming out of Pegasus's loose box and went over. "What do you think about Spartan, then?" she asked, trying to sound casual as she caressed Pegasus's face.

Ty bolted the door. "You really want to know?"

Amy nodded.

"I don't like the look of him," Ty said seriously. "You watch yourself, Amy."

Amy surprised herself by jumping to Spartan's defence. "He's not *really* bad," she said quickly. "You should have seen him before the accident, when Mom and I went to get him. He was so gentle."

"Well, not any more." Ty shook his head. "There's that

look in his eyes. It makes me wonder if he's been through too much to be cured."

"He'll settle," Amy said uneasily. "He'll get better." She said the words automatically, feeling a desperate need to believe in them herself. If Spartan didn't get better what would it mean for her? She knew she wouldn't be able to deal with him being put to sleep. She *had* to make him better.

Chapter Three

Amy was busy enough for the next few hours to keep her mind off Spartan. She brought Raisin, the younger of the two new show-jumpers, out of the barn with a halter and long-line on.

Raisin was a pretty chestnut who panicked and tried to bolt every time a rider attempted to mount her. In all other respects – being groomed, handled and led, etc. – the mare was obedient and responsive, and Amy was sure that her problem could be cured.

As she led the chestnut up to the circular ring by the turn-out paddocks, Lou came jogging up the yard. "What are you going to do with Raisin today?" she asked with interest.

"I'm going to join-up with her," Amy said. Joining-up was a way of establishing a relationship of trust and understanding with the horse. It was a technique Marion had taught Amy.

"Can I watch?" Lou asked.

"Sure," Amy said.

When they reached the circular ring Lou leant against the fence. After shutting the gate behind them, Amy rubbed Raisin's forehead with the flat of her hand and then un-clipped the long-line. She tossed one end towards the horse's hindquarters. With a slight jump of surprise, Raisin trotted away. Moving quickly so that her shoulders were square with Raisin's, Amy pitched the long-line again. With a snort, the chestnut broke into a high-headed canter.

By keeping her shoulders square to Raisin's body and her eyes fixed on the mare's eyes Amy urged her on. After seven circuits she stepped slightly to the front of the horse, blocking her movement and sending her at a canter in the opposite direction.

"Look," she said to Lou after another few circuits. "See her ear?" Raisin's inside ear was pointing into the circle in Amy's direction. "It means she's ready."

She urged the mare on a few more times, waiting patiently for the next signal. At last it came. Raisin slowed to a trot and started to lick and chew with her mouth. This was the way a horse showed that it wanted to be friends. Then came the final signal. Raisin stretched out her head and neck so that her muzzle was almost on the floor.

In one swift movement, Amy turned her shoulders side-ways on to the horse and dropped her eyes, concentrating entirely on Raisin and forgetting about Lou's steady gaze on her. Out of the corner of her eye she saw Raisin slow to a stop. The horse stared at Amy and then decisively walked into the middle of the circle up to Amy's back, stopping by her shoulder and snorting softly. It was the moment of joining-up!

Amy turned slowly and rubbed Raisin's forehead. "Good girl," she murmured before walking away. To Raisin, as to all horses, humans were predators, but by moving away with non-aggressive body language, Amy was telling her that she was no threat. What she wanted now was for Raisin to voluntarily choose to be with her, to follow her. To her delight, as she moved across the ring the chestnut did exactly that – her nose by Amy's shoulder, her warm breath on Amy's neck. At last Amy stopped and rewarded her with another rub on the forehead.

"Now we've got an understanding," Amy told Lou, "I can start working on getting her used to being mounted. She'll be much easier to handle now."

To prove her point, she ran her palms over Raisin's back and then eased her weight on to her hands. Raisin didn't flinch. Amy stroked her. "That's enough for today," she said.

Lou's eyes shone as she opened the gate. "That was incredible!"

Amy nodded. She had watched her mom on numerous occasions and understood exactly how Lou was feeling. "No matter how many times you do it, it never feels any less amazing," she said.

"So, are you going to join-up with Spartan?" Lou asked curiously as they led Raisin down the yard.

Ty, who was walking past with a water-bucket, stopped. "It would be crazy at this stage," he said, looking at Amy. "There's no knowing what he might do."

"He's not *that* bad," Amy protested, knowing deep down that Ty was right.

"He could be dangerous," Ty said, his dark eyes serious.

"He's not," Amy retorted, seeing the look of concern on her sister's face. She turned to Ty. "Look, relax. I wasn't thinking about joining-up with him just yet. He'd probably try and jump out of the ring right now."

"Or worse," Ty said.

Amy ignored him. "I thought I'd just try and get him used to me first by going into his stall." She swallowed. "I've decided to start this afternoon."

As Amy approached Spartan's stall after lunch, she realized that never before had she experienced such a reluctant feeling about working with a horse. He stared warily at her, his head high, his long black forelock tumbling down over his handsome dished face. Amy hesitated. Although she was nervous, her natural instinct was to walk straight up to his door. She needed to get close to him, to make him realize that he had nothing to fear.

She took a step forward.

Immediately, Spartan threw his head up and half reared.

Amy stopped in her tracks, frozen by indecision.

Maybe, she thought, *if I just stand here, he'll calm down in a minute and let me get closer. But then, I might just be causing him unnecessary stress.*

She waited, but Spartan didn't calm down. He paced from foot to foot, his head held high. After several long minutes, Amy fetched a chair from the tack-room and placed it directly in front of the loose box. Spartan moved ceaselessly, side to side, backwards and forwards.

An hour passed. Amy stood up and tried to move the chair a little closer but Spartan reared violently. Amy decided to give it a break — maybe she'd have more luck tomorrow. As she returned the chair to the tack-room, she couldn't help worrying that she wouldn't have any luck at all. *Perhaps I should just ring Scott and tell him that this isn't going to work*, she thought.

Spartan was looking out over his door when she walked back to the stable block. She paused, down-wind of him. He was looking out across the fields, unaware of her. His ears were pricked and for one fleeting moment, she saw the beautiful, intelligent horse that he had been before the accident.

Amy stepped forward. Spartan heard her footstep and swung round. His eyes fixed on her and in that moment a terrible knowledge seemed to flow between them — a shared memory of that horrific night. With a snort, Spartan plunged back into his stall.

Amy stood rooted to the spot. Suddenly she knew that she wasn't going to ring Scott – she couldn't. Like it or not, she and Spartan were bound together. However much he hated her, she was the only one that could understand what he had been through and who had the power to relieve his pain.

That evening, while Amy and Lou were cleaning up after supper, the phone rang. Amy answered it and then handed it over to Lou. "It's for you. It's Carl."

Lou took the phone eagerly. "Carl!"

Amy switched the TV on and collapsed into an armchair. In the background she heard Lou tell Carl everything that had been going on. After a while there was a pause. "Yes, I miss you too," Lou said into the phone. "I can't wait to see you again. Only two more days to go now."

Amy rolled her eyes.

Then Lou's tone changed slightly. "I can't come back yet. You know I'm needed here at the moment, Carl." There was a pause and then her voice took on just the faintest tinge of irritation. "I don't know when," she said. "Yes, I know I said the end of the summer, but..." She broke off. "Of course I want to be with you but at the moment I have to stay at Heartland." She looked round and saw Amy watching her. She lowered her voice. "Look, we can talk about this when you get here."

Amy turned back to the television.

"How's Carl?" Grandpa asked as Lou put the phone down. "Fine, he's..."

"Hey, look! I don't believe it!" Amy sat up suddenly in her chair, interrupting Lou. "There's a commercial for Green Briar on TV!"

Green Briar was a large livery and competition yard not far from Heartland. Val Grant, Green Briar's owner, was standing in front of a newly-painted eighteen-stall barn, smiling broadly at the camera.

Grandpa and Lou came and stood behind the armchair.

"Want a perfect pony?" the voice-over on the TV asked as the camera shot changed to show a couple of beautiful ponies cantering around a course of jumps. "A pony who'll win you ribbons?"

Amy scowled. She knew all about the forceful techniques that Val Grant used to make her ponies canter so correctly, heads poised, hooves snapping up precisely as they cleared a jump.

The camera zoomed in closer on one of the riders. "It's Ashley!" Amy exclaimed.

Ashley Grant was fifteen and she and Amy were in the same class at school. The pony she was riding cantered smoothly towards a jump. Ashley's immaculate breeches clung to her slim legs, her sleek blonde hair was tied back in a ponytail and her face was beautifully made-up. Her pony jumped the fence perfectly and she brought it to a halt, smiling straight into the camera.

"If you've ever dreamt of owning a perfect pony," the voice said as the camera cut to a shot of Val Grant stroking a pony with a blue ribbon fluttering on his bridle, "then come to Green Briar. The place where dreams really *can* come true."

"Gross!" Amy exclaimed as the music faded out and the next advert came on. She turned to Grandpa and Lou indignantly. "The whole thing's just aimed at people who want ribbon-winning, push-button ponies!"

Grandpa nodded in agreement, but Lou was looking at the TV thoughtfully. "You know, that's not a bad idea – making an advert," she said. "Maybe we should consider it. Talking of which…" she snapped off the TV. "Grandpa, Amy, it's time I told you about the plans I've been making for Heartland."

"Ah yes, your plans to make us more profitable," Grandpa said.

"Yes," Lou said briskly. "Now don't look at me like that," she said, obviously seeing Amy's face cloud over. "When it comes to business I know what I'm talking about. It's what I'm good at." She fetched a pile of papers. "First of all," she said, "it's obvious that we need to raise more money. Before the winter the roof on the barn is going to need fixing, and there'll be other expenses – rugs, extra hay and straw. In addition, I feel that we need to maximize Heartland's potential."

"Stop talking like you're in a business meeting, Lou!" Amy protested.

"But this place *is* a business." Before Amy had a chance to say anything more, Lou continued. "Now, my first idea to raise funds for the winter: I thought we could hold a barn dance."

"A barn dance!" Jack Bartlett echoed.

"Don't look like that, Grandpa," Lou chided. "A dance is an ideal way to raise money. We get a band, provide food and drink and then charge for the tickets as well as having a raffle. This place is plenty big enough," she said.

"But who would come?" Amy blurted out.

"Mom's friends," Lou said. "It would be the ideal opportunity to invite them up here. I think they've been staying away to give us enough time..." She trailed off for a moment. "It would be a way of breaking the ice – of showing them that we don't want them to stay away any more. And it's a cause they'd support."

"But Lou, are you sure it would work?" Jack Bartlett ran a hand through his hair. "It sounds expensive – a band, food, prizes for the raffle. How would we pay for all that?"

"Well, there would be the money from the tickets and we'd ask people to help out and donate things. Everyone has always been willing to help Heartland in the past, haven't they?" Grandpa nodded. "Well, they will again now," Lou said. "The whole idea is that it costs us very little but that we make a substantial amount of money."

"What if people don't come?" Amy said. She was finding it hard to imagine their family friends coming to a dance where they had to pay for tickets.

"They will!" Lou insisted. She looked round. "Well, what do you say?"

"OK, I guess," Grandpa said tentatively.

"Great!" Lou said. "I'll start organizing it – we'll have it in two weeks' time. The sooner the better."

"Two weeks!" Amy said.

Lou waved a hand. "That gives me enough time, no problem. Carl will help out when he gets here. I'll start ringing round straight away."

Amy frowned. She didn't have a good feeling about this dance. It just didn't seem right to her.

Lou straightened up her papers. Amy noticed that for the first time in ages she looked in her element. "Now let's look at some ways of increasing Heartland's profits. Obviously the bulk of our money comes from the paying-horses – the non-residents who come here to have their problems solved. I think we need to market ourselves more effectively in order to get the maximum number of customers." She pulled out a piece of paper. "So, I propose that we have some sort of brochure that we can distribute in tack shops, feed merchants – basically anywhere that horsy people go. Have a look at this outline."

Amy could see that the piece of paper she was holding was split into three sections. There was a column with the title HEARTLAND in big letters, and suggestions for several photographs. The next column described Heartland's work, and gave quotes from a recent magazine article and AS RECOMMENDED BY NICK HALLIWELL in large letters across it;

and the final section detailed the services Heartland offered and the fees that were charged. Amy's heart sank. Lou just didn't understand what Heartland was about. Mom had never given estimates! She had always had a flexible system for charging people, avoiding set fees because of her belief that every horse was an individual and needed a different approach. A couple of lines on the plan caught Amy's eye:

> *At Heartland we offer a unique deal — for $50 we will assess your horse's needs and provide a detailed written evaluation.*

"No," Amy said, shaking her head. She pointed at the offending paragraph.

"What's the matter?" Lou asked.

"We're not going to start evaluating horses and charging people for it. No way!"

"Why not?" Lou said. "It's perfectly normal. If you want someone to do some work for you, you get a quote first and then decide whether you want to pursue it."

"But how can we?" Amy exclaimed. "You can't tell how long a horse is going to take to be cured until you start working with it — and even then you may have setbacks or things might not go as planned. Mom *never* charged people until after the treatment."

"People expect a quote," Lou said. "It's a more professional approach…"

"Well, I'm not doing it!" Amy interrupted. "I don't want to change things. Everything worked just fine for Mom."

"Everything could have worked *better*," Lou said. She shook her head, looking upset. "Amy, I'm only trying to help. We don't *have* to carry on doings things exactly the way Mom did. We can make changes so things are easier for us around here."

"No, we can't!" Amy said, her voice rising as panic took hold of her. She didn't want there to be changes. She wanted things to stay just the way Mom had left them. "You can forget it, Lou! Forget this whole stupid brochure idea!" She jumped to her feet.

"Come on, Amy," Grandpa put in. "Sit down and let's discuss it calmly."

"No!" Amy said. She stormed to the door and slammed it behind her. Fighting a tide of panic she hurried up to her bedroom. She couldn't let Lou change things! That just couldn't happen!

Opening her door, she immediately focused on the photograph of her mom on her dressing-table. She walked over and picked it up. "Oh, Mom," she whispered desperately. "Why aren't you here?"

Chapter Four

The next morning the atmosphere in the kitchen was tense. Amy's sleep had been disturbed by nightmares again. She felt groggy with lack of sleep and depressed by the argument of the day before. She scowled at Lou as she sat down at the table.

"Can you pass the milk, please?" Lou asked.

Amy handed her the carton, banging it down on the table. She got up again, brushing past Lou to get to the kettle.

"Amy!" Lou said angrily as Amy knocked her arm.

"Oh, come on you two," Jack Bartlett said with a sigh. "How about a compromise?" he paused. "We still consider the brochure idea, Lou, but maybe you can re-work it and then discuss it again with Amy."

"But it doesn't need re-working, Grandpa!" Lou protested. "I really do think it's fine as it is..."

"Compromise," Grandpa said firmly.

"OK," Lou sighed. "I'll take another look at it." She looked at Amy. "But the dance *is* going ahead."

Grandpa nodded. "Yes. The dance can go ahead and Amy and I will give you all the help you need." He threw Amy a warning glance as she opened her mouth to object. "Won't we, Amy?"

"I guess," she muttered.

"Good," said Grandpa with a smile. "Now, can we just get on with being civilized to one another, *please?*"

In the middle of the morning, Scott's old Chevy came chugging up the driveway. Amy hurried down the yard to meet him. "Hi there," he said to her, getting out. "I was just passing and thought I'd stop by."

Lou was walking across the yard with an armful of fresh grass. She stopped. "Hello, Scott."

Scott smiled, looking at the grass in her arms. "For Sugarfoot?"

"Yes," Lou said. "I gave him some yesterday and he loved it. Are you going to come and see him?"

Scott joined her. As they walked off up the yard, Amy overheard Lou telling him about her plans for the barn dance.

"That sounds great!" Scott said, obviously impressed. "You can put me down for a ticket! I'll spread the word, too. After all, it's in a good cause."

"Brilliant!" Lou said, her eyes shining. "Thanks, Scott."

Amy felt surprised — she wouldn't have thought Scott would have been interested in something like a dance. Maybe she was just being unreasonable and it was a good idea after all. Yawning, she went into the tack-room.

Ty was cleaning a bridle. He looked up as Amy collected a grooming bucket. "Who are you going to groom?"

"Spartan," Amy said.

"Are you sure?" Ty asked.

"It's now or never," Amy said resolutely.

As she opened Spartan's door he plunged forward. But Amy moved quicker. She closed in on his head, quickly snapping a lead-rope on to his halter. Feeling her hand near his face, Spartan panicked. He rose up on his back legs and his front hooves came crashing down. Still Amy held on, staying close beside him and moving up to his head the second his hooves hit the ground. Eyes rolling, Spartan reluctantly submitted to the control of the halter and rope.

"Easy now," Amy soothed, picking up a grooming brush.

Spartan started in alarm. His body language told her that he didn't want her in his stall. He didn't want her holding his head and he didn't want her trying to brush him. With determination, Amy lifted the brush to his coat. He flinched as if she had hit him.

Amy sighed. She knew she should keep trying to groom Spartan, be firm but kind with him, keep persisting, but she just couldn't bear to inflict further stress on the horse. She put the brush back in the bucket. Maybe she would just take him out to graze instead.

Keeping a watchful eye on him, she led him out of his stall and over to a large patch of grass in front of the house. He snorted, moving beside her with high, nervous steps. Amy stopped him at the grass but he didn't lower his neck. Instead, he stood with every muscle tensed and his eyes fixed on her.

Ty came over.

"I was hoping he might relax and eat a bit of grass," Amy explained. "But it doesn't look like he's going to."

"Do you want me to hold him for a bit?" Ty offered.

"OK," Amy said.

Ty took the lead-rope.

Once Spartan was satisfied that Amy was at a safe distance he put his head down and jerkily started to snatch at the grass. Amy wiped the sweat off her forehead with the back of her hand.

Ty looked over. "Give it time," he said quietly.

Amy nodded. Ty always seemed to understand how she was feeling when it came to horses. They worked really well together. Standing in silence, they watched Spartan graze.

After a while, Scott came down the yard with Lou. "How's Spartan doing?" he asked, looking at the bay horse.

Amy wondered what to say. How could she admit to Scott that she wasn't making any progress? What would he think? "He's OK," she said quickly.

"Great," Scott smiled. "Well, keep up the good work."

As he turned and walked off towards his Chevy, Amy caught Ty giving her a puzzled look. To her relief he didn't say anything. She watched Scott drive away and then sighed. "I'd better take Spartan back in now," she said.

"Sure," Ty replied.

Amy took the lead-rope from him and Spartan pulled back in alarm. "Easy now!" Amy soothed, but the horse threw up his head wildly. Amy moved in beside him and tightened her grip. "Walk on," she said, clicking her tongue.

As Spartan reluctantly stepped forward beside her, Amy could sense fierce hatred pulsating through every muscle and nerve in his body.

Ty opened Spartan's stall door for Amy. Lou came over, looking apprehensively at the bay horse. "How is he?" she asked.

"Fine," Amy said curtly. She led Spartan into his stall and automatically unclipped his lead-rope. It was the opportunity Spartan had been waiting for.

Free at last, he threw himself towards Amy, the full force of his body cannoning into her and knocking her over to the wall. She stumbled, and heard Lou scream and Ty shout out her name as Spartan swung his hindquarters towards her. Amy was too quick for him, though. Scrambling to her feet, she flung herself towards his head. Her fingers fumbled for the halter. Grasping the leather, she brought his head round and backed him into a corner until he was under control again. For a moment she stood there, clutching his halter, her heart pounding.

"Amy! Get out of the stall!" Lou cried.

Amy looked round to see Lou and Ty staring at her in shock.

She led Spartan over to the door, only letting go of him when she could slip safely out. Then she let out a shaky breath.

Lou grabbed her by the shoulders. "Amy! You could have been badly hurt!"

"It was nothing." Amy pulled back, her hands still trembling slightly. She glanced back at the box, not wanting either of them to blame Spartan. "It was stupid of me. I should never have unclipped his rope like that."

"But he tried to kill you!" Lou exclaimed.

"He did not!" Amy protested. She shook her head, angry at herself. "I should have been more careful."

"More careful!" Lou exclaimed. "That horse is dangerous, Amy! He needs to be put down!"

"What?" Amy gasped.

"He's not safe," cried Lou.

Anger surged through Amy. "What would you know?" she cried, drawing herself up. "You're an expert all of a sudden, are you?" She saw Lou's face stiffen but was too upset to stop herself. "You don't know what you're talking about, Lou!" she shouted. "Just stay out of it!"

Lou went pale and then turned swiftly away.

There was a moment's pause then Ty cleared his throat. "That was a bit harsh, Amy."

Amy swung round. "She shouldn't have said that!"

"She's only concerned about you," Ty said. "You shouldn't have spoken to her like that."

Amy felt her cheeks flame with guilt and humiliation. "She's my sister. I can speak to her how I want. Keep out of it, Ty!"

"Fine," Ty said shortly. "If that's how you feel." He turned and walked off.

As Amy watched him disappear out of sight, her temper suddenly faded as quickly as it had flared up. "*Great*," she muttered, throwing the lead-rope down. "Just great!"

From the end of the row of stalls there was a snort. Amy looked round and saw Pegasus watching her. "Oh, Pegasus," she groaned, walking over to him. Pegasus nuzzled her hair. Amy stroked his neck and felt her raging emotions gradually ebb away. She sighed. She knew what she had to do.

Taking a deep breath she went up the yard. Ty was sweeping near the muck heap. He must have heard her footsteps because he glanced up. Seeing it was her, he concentrated on his sweeping again.

"I'm sorry, Ty," Amy said.

Ty leant on the yard brush and looked at her.

"I shouldn't have said those things," Amy said. "I ... I just lost it."

"It's OK," Ty said with a shrug.

"It's not," Amy said quickly. "I didn't mean them." She rubbed her forehead. "Everything's just getting to me at the moment. I haven't been sleeping well. I'm sorry, Ty – really I am."

Ty's face softened. "Look, forget it."

Amy breathed a sigh of relief. She hated it when Ty was mad at her. "Thanks," she said gratefully.

He picked up the brush again. "So are you going to apologize to Lou, then?"

"After she said those things about Spartan?" Amy protested. "What does she know anyway?"

Ty shrugged. "Maybe not that much." He glanced up. "But she does care about you, Amy."

"No way!" she said, reading his expression. "I am *not* going to apologize to her. She saw Ty's eyebrows raise. "I'm not!"

Chapter Five

As the hours passed, Amy began to feel guilty about the way she had treated Lou — but she still couldn't bring herself to apologize. Every time she thought about Spartan being put down she felt like she wanted to be sick.

Amy avoided going into the farmhouse all day until she couldn't put it off any longer. She said goodnight to the horses and walked reluctantly down to the back door.

Lou was setting the table.

As Amy walked in and their eyes met, she turned away and kicked off her trainers. She waited for her sister to tell her to put them away, but Lou didn't say a word.

Amy fetched a Coke from the fridge and glanced across at Lou who was placing the three sets of knives and forks down, each metal piece making a dull thud against the table. Her face was pale.

Amy suddenly couldn't bear the atmosphere any longer. "Lou..."

Lou looked up at her.

"I shouldn't have said those things," Amy said quickly. "I'm sorry. I didn't mean to hurt you."

Lou's face softened. "Oh, Amy," she said, stepping forward. "I was just so worried about you—"

Lou broke off quickly as Jack Bartlett came into the kitchen.

"Hi, honey," he said to Amy. Then he frowned. "I hear you had a bit of a problem with Spartan today."

Amy's eyes shot to Lou, who looked away, her cheeks flushing.

"Amy?" Jack Bartlett prompted.

"Well, not really," Amy lied desperately, her mind racing. Why had Lou told Grandpa? If he thought Spartan was dangerous he would stop her working with him. "He was just a bit excitable," she said quickly. "Nothing really bad."

"He tried to attack you, Amy!" Lou said.

"He did not!" Amy exclaimed. "You're exaggerating!"

"You know I'm not!" Lou cried back at her.

"That's enough!" Grandpa shouted, slamming his fist down on the kitchen table.

Amy and Lou glared at each other.

Jack Bartlett looked from one to the other. "If he's that dangerous, Amy..."

"He isn't!" Amy interrupted. "Grandpa, he just needs help!"

Her grandpa looked at her for a moment as if he was

going to say something and then to Amy's relief he let the matter drop and turned to deal with the stew bubbling on the top of the stove. Amy scowled at Lou and stomped past her to go and get changed.

The next morning, when Amy came downstairs, Lou was busy making out an invitation list for the dance.

"Morning, Grandpa," Amy yawned, shaking out a couple of painkillers from a bottle on the sideboard. She had been awake since four o'clock and her head ached.

"Are you OK?" Jack Bartlett asked, looking at her in concern.

Amy nodded.

Lou looked up from her notepad. "We need to decide on the food for the dance," she declared. "I thought we might have a barbecue, then all we need to do is get a load of steaks, some chicken and some corn on the cob and that's most of the food done. What do you think?"

"Sounds great," Grandpa said. He turned. "What do you think Amy?"

Amy shrugged. "Whatever."

"That leaves the desserts." Lou looked straight at Amy. "But I won't bother telling you about those. You don't seem to be the least bit interested in trying to save Heartland."

"Stop it!" Grandpa said. "This arguing has gone on long enough." He looked from one to the other. "Now listen, both of you, how about we take a trip to the cinema on Sunday?

It would do us all good to get out for the day and I'd like to see you enjoy being together for a change. What do you say?"

"Sure," Amy shrugged.

"Fine," Lou said flippantly. "Carl might still be here, so he can come too."

"Oh, great," Amy muttered under her breath.

Lou looked at her sharply. "What was that?"

Amy caught Grandpa's warning look. "Nothing," she sighed. She walked to the door. "I'm going to feed the horses."

Straight after breakfast Lou set off to collect Carl from the airport. After finishing the other stalls with Ty, Amy went to see Spartan. She was again attempting to groom him when a shadow fell across the door. Amy glanced round.

Her grandpa was standing there. "Hey there," he said.

"Hi," Amy said, her heart sinking. She didn't want Grandpa there in case Spartan misbehaved.

To her horror, he unbolted the door and came in. Spartan instinctively shrank back.

"It's OK," Amy murmured, stroking his neck.

But Spartan lashed out at her with his front hoof, narrowly missing her hand as she moved hastily away. She saw her grandfather frown.

"Why did he do that?" he asked.

"He doesn't like me touching him," Amy said quietly.

Jack Bartlett shook his head, looking at Spartan's flattened ears and rolling eyes. "I don't have a good feeling about him, Amy."

"He'll be fine," Amy insisted. "He's just traumatized. I'm going to make him better."

Jack Bartlett sighed. "Amy, honey, not every horse can be helped, even your mom used to admit that," he said, coming up close. "Sometimes, hard though it is, it's best to just accept that there isn't..."

"No," Amy interrupted him, not wanting to listen to what she knew he was going to say. As if aware that she was momentarily distracted, Spartan suddenly jerked his neck upwards. Amy jumped back as she saw his head swing round. But Grandpa wasn't so fast. Spartan's teeth sank into his arm.

Amy's grandfather let out a yell of pain. Slowed by shock, Amy grabbed out at Spartan's halter – too late.

"My arm!" Grandpa exclaimed. Spartan's teeth had left an ugly red welt on the skin.

"Grandpa, I'm sorry!" Amy gasped. Her eyes shot to Spartan. He was standing, unrepentant, with his ears still back. She followed her grandpa as he hurriedly let himself out of the stall. "It was a mistake," she said, her eyes filling with tears. "He didn't mean it." Behind her, Spartan's hooves crashed into the wall of his stall. "Please, Grandpa, he really didn't."

She followed Jack Bartlett as he strode silently down to the house holding his arm. In the kitchen, Amy watched as he fetched the first aid kit and bathed the bite. She felt horribly guilty. "I'll get some arnica cream," she offered, desperate to find something she could do to help. "It will help the bruising."

Amy hurried up the yard to the cabinet in the feed-room where all the natural remedies were kept, and returned with the cream.

Grandpa applied it to his arm. His face was serious. As he screwed the top back on the jar he looked directly at Amy, speaking quietly but firmly. "This can't go on, Amy. He's going to really hurt someone one of these days."

Amy swallowed. "He won't, Grandpa. He's going to get better. He just needs more time."

"I'd like to believe you, but I can't." Grandpa sighed. "I think…" But before he could say what he thought there was the sound of a car stopping outside the house. Amy looked out of the window. "It's Lou and Carl!" Relief flooded through her as the car doors opened. She knew the arrival would distract Grandpa for the meantime.

"We'll talk about this later," Grandpa said, heading towards the door.

Carl was standing by the car looking round, his dark hair immaculate, his eyes hidden by shades. To Amy's surprise she saw that he was wearing jeans, a leather belt with a big buckle and sturdy boots. For some reason she had expected him to be wearing a suit like the one she had seen him in before. She glanced at his clothes – they looked new and expensive, but he'd obviously made an effort to dress casually.

Lou came round the front of the car. "You remember Grandpa and Amy, don't you, Carl?" she said happily.

"Of course I do." Carl smiled at Amy and then stepped forward, holding out his hand to Grandpa. "Pleased to meet you again, Jack."

"Did you have a good flight?" Jack Bartlett asked.

Carl nodded. "Not bad." He looked round. "This place is neat."

Jack Bartlett smiled. "Well, we like it. Why don't you bring your stuff in and Lou can show you around?"

"Yeah, sure." He pulled out a green and beige overnight bag from the back of the car, shrugged it on to his shoulder and followed Grandpa and Lou into the house.

Amy didn't go with them. She was feeling confused. Carl actually seemed quite pleasant: it wasn't how she remembered him at all. She walked up to Pegasus's box and stroked him thoughtfully.

After a while, Carl and Lou came out of the house. "This is Pegasus," Lou said as they got close. "He was Daddy's horse. He was one of the top show-jumpers in the world ... until the accident." Carl stepped forward towards the horse. "He can be a bit nervous of strangers," Lou warned quickly. "You have to be careful about how you approach him."

Carl laughed confidently. "I know how to approach a horse. I used to spend hours playing with my cousin's pony when we were kids. Hello, big fella!" he said, his hand reaching out to pat Pegasus firmly on the forehead. "How you doing?"

Alarmed by the hand banging down on his forehead, Pegasus shot backwards into his stall with a snort.

"Hey!" Carl exclaimed, looking startled.

Amy frowned. "You should never approach a horse like that! I thought you said you knew about horses?"

"Of course I do," Carl said sharply. "That horse is just bad-tempered."

How would you like it if a stranger marched up to you and slapped you between the eyes? Amy felt like exclaiming.

Carl turned to Lou. "Right, what needs doing? That one over there looks like it could do with a groom." He walked towards Spartan. "Hi there, boy!"

Spartan snaked his head forward.

"I think we'll leave Spartan," Lou said, grabbing Carl's arm and steering him away. "But there's a pony at the top that I want you to meet."

"Lead me to him," Carl said. "Just you tell me how I can help."

Lou looked at Amy. "We'll go and do that, OK? We'll be up with Sugarfoot."

Amy nodded. As she watched them walk up the yard towards the back barn, she heard Carl say, "Ah, yes, this takes me back." She frowned to herself. Carl obviously didn't know anything about horses so why was he pretending he did?

Matt rang that afternoon. "Hi. How you doing?"

"OK," Amy told him. "Carl's here."

"How's that going?" Matt asked.

Amy frowned. "I'm not sure. He obviously doesn't know anything about horses but he's pretending that he does. I think he's just trying to please Lou."

"What's wrong with that?" Matt said, sounding mystified.

"I don't know..." Amy struggled to explain. "It's just that he's sort of trying too hard."

"Yeah," Matt said, not sounding like he understood. He paused. "Do you want to go and see a film this week?"

Amy sighed. "I can't. It's really busy round here, with Carl here and Lou trying to get everything ready for the dance. And Carl's taking us out for dinner tonight. Why don't you come by here some time instead?"

"Sure, OK," Matt said. "I'll see you soon."

The kitchen door opened as Amy put the phone down. Lou and Carl came in, hand in hand. "Hi!" Lou said, her eyes shining. "I was hoping you'd be here. Carl's been having some great ideas to make Heartland more profitable."

"What sort of ideas?" Amy said.

Carl sat down. "Just ways to help this place make money." He put his arms around Lou's waist and pulled her close.

Lou giggled and bent down to kiss the top of his head. "It's great to have you here," she said to him.

Amy pulled a face and headed towards the door.

"Don't you want to hear what we've got to say?" Lou said, sounding hurt. "We thought that there could be an 'adopt a horse' campaign. You know — people pay a certain amount and get a photo of a horse and a newsletter?"

Amy shook her head. "It wouldn't work. We re-home all the horses we can, we don't have enough permanent residents for something like that."

"Oh," Lou said, the sparkle fading from her eyes.

"Look, I'm going back out to the yard," Amy said quickly, turning away to avoid any further discussion.

Over the meal in the restaurant that night, Lou and Carl told Grandpa and Amy about the other ideas they had come up with. Jack Bartlett listened and nodded while Amy tried to suppress the tension she felt rising inside her. Lou was obviously really happy to have Carl around and Amy didn't want to ruin the evening. She was even beginning to think that maybe she should try to *like* Carl, for Lou's sake. But when Lou explained Carl's suggestion to limit the number of stalls kept for rescue horses to five and use all the other stalls for horses whose owners paid to have them cured, Amy couldn't restrain herself any longer.

"What?" she exclaimed loudly. Some of the other people in the restaurant looked over. Amy lowered her voice. "What are you thinking of, Lou?"

"It makes sense," Lou said. "The paying horses would

support the cost of looking after the rescued horses and we'd make a profit."

"We're not reducing the number of rescue horses!" Amy said. "In fact, we're not making any changes." Her throat felt tight. "Everything's got to stay just as Mom left it. No changes." Her head was aching. She saw Grandpa look at her and open his mouth to speak. "No changes!" she repeated. Suddenly she couldn't bear to be at the table any longer. She got to her feet and hurried to the toilets. To her relief they were empty.

Amy looked at herself in the mirror. Her face was pale and her grey eyes were ringed with purple shadows from lack of sleep. Thoughts whirled around in her head — Lou and Carl, Spartan, changes to Heartland, Mom...

Shutting her eyes, she leant her forehead against the cold glass, wishing she could be somewhere — anywhere — else.

As always, the nightmares came back that night. The creaking of the tree and the rain, the wind and the thunder ringing in her ears, and the sight of the tree falling. When Amy switched on the light it was three-thirty in the morning. She sat up, waiting for the feeling of panic to subside.

Taking a deep breath, she picked up a magazine from the floor. Pulling the bedclothes up around her she started leafing through it. She had been reading for about half an hour when her bedroom door creaked open. Her eyes shot up. Grandpa was standing in the doorway, looking concerned.

"Amy?" he said in a low voice. "It's four o'clock in the morning. What's your light doing on?"

"I ... I couldn't sleep," she said.

His face softened and he came and sat down beside her. "Did you have that bad dream again?"

Amy nodded.

Jack Bartlett looked at her for a moment and then stroked her hair. "Night-time is always the worst even without the dreams, isn't it?" he said softly. "I have nights when I lie awake thinking about why I let you and your mom go out in that storm. Why didn't I stop you?"

Amy stared at him in surprise. "But it wasn't *your* fault, Grandpa!"

"I know that," he said. "Deep down, I know that *nothing* could have stopped your mom going out that night once she'd decided to – just as nothing could have made her go if she hadn't wanted to. But grief's like that..." His eyes searched Amy's. "You always feel you could have done more. You always blame yourself."

Amy swallowed as Grandpa leant over and hugged her. "It *will* get easier in time, honey," he said. "I promise you it will." He cradled her in his arms, rocking her back and forth.

Amy shut her eyes tightly. Her throat ached with unshed tears. *Was he right?* She knew that he had nothing to blame himself for, but what about her? She had pleaded with Mom to go out that night. His words ran round in her head: *Nothing could have made her go if she hadn't wanted to.* She wished desperately that she could believe those words — *really* believe them.

Although Carl had only planned to come for an overnight visit he decided to stay the following day as well. By the evening, Amy was longing for him to go. As far as she was concerned, his interest in everything was very obviously just an act. Amy couldn't believe that Lou didn't see through it. Lou seemed to be oblivious, though, delighted to have someone around who would take her ideas seriously for a change.

When Amy came in from finishing off with the horses for the night she found Carl and Lou in the kitchen, dressed up as if ready to go out. "Put your shoes away," Lou automatically reminded her.

Stubbornly, Amy kicked her trainers into a corner. She was tired and could do without Lou's nagging. "We need some more feed, Lou," she said abruptly.

"I've ordered some," Lou said. "It's arriving on Monday."

Amy looked at her in surprise. "But McCullochs don't deliver on Monday."

"We're not using McCullochs any more," Lou said. "They're really expensive. Carl and I were looking into it this afternoon. Rathmores do a pony cube for half the price so I've decided that we'll use them in the future."

Amy stared at her in disbelief. "You've what?" she said.

"I've decided that we'll use Rathmores," Lou repeated. "They're delivering on Monday."

"It seems an excellent idea," Carl said. "It'll be so much more economical."

"It won't!" Amy exclaimed. "You'll have to cancel the order, Lou. Rathmores' food is second-rate. If we use it, we'll have to feed twice as much! We won't save money, the horses' health will suffer because it's not such good quality, and it'll be hopeless for the horses that have digestive upsets. They'll be far more likely to get colic and to suffer from allergic reactions. We just can't feed it."

"I didn't realize," Lou said, her face suddenly falling.

"So why didn't you ask?" Amy cried in frustration.

"It seemed like such a good idea at the time," Lou said defensively. "Anyway, you never have the time of day to listen to me, Amy!"

"Can't you see why?" Amy exploded. "Look what a mess you've made of something as straightforward as this!"

A little later, she heard the sound of the back door opening. She looked out of her bedroom window and saw Lou and Carl walking towards Lou's car. They were laughing together. Amy suddenly realized that she hadn't seen Lou laugh like that in ages. Doubt flickered in her mind. Was she wrong to dislike Carl so much? He obviously made Lou happy.

Amy struggled with her thoughts as she watched them get into the car. She wanted Lou to be happy and yet she just couldn't repress the uncomfortable feelings she had about Carl. She sighed. Maybe she should make more of an effort.

After all, she wanted Lou to stay at Heartland – even if it meant Carl being around a lot. It would be hard but she'd try.

The next morning, Amy was drinking coffee with Grandpa when Lou came down for breakfast alone.

"Hi," Amy greeted her sister, remembering the decision she had made the night before.

Lou smiled faintly.

"Did you have a good time last night?" Jack Bartlett asked.

"Yes, thank you," Lou said, her voice subdued.

Jack Bartlett looked closely at her. "Lou? Is there something the matter?"

"No," Lou replied. She sat down at the table and started fiddling with a pen, turning it round and round in her fingers. "Well, not *exactly*." She suddenly put the pen down and taking a deep breath, looked at them both. "I guess you might as well know. Carl has got a new job in Chicago and he's asked me to go with him."

Amy stared at her in astonishment. "But you're not going to, are you? Chicago's miles away!"

Lou didn't say anything.

"Lou?" Grandpa said.

"I've told him I'll think about it," Lou replied at last. "But I think ... I think I might say yes."

Chapter Six

Amy followed Lou up to the feed-room. Despite their arguments she desperately wanted Lou to stay at Heartland. They had spent so much of their lives apart since Lou had begged to be allowed to stay on at her English boarding school and Marion and Amy had moved to Virginia to live with Grandpa. Amy felt that she was just starting to get to know her older sister and she didn't want her to leave.

"You're not really going to go to Chicago, are you?" she asked. "What would you do there?"

"I'd get a job," Lou said, setting out the feed buckets. "I might even be able to transfer with my present company."

"But you'd be going there just to be with Carl?" Amy said.

"Yes." Lou looked suddenly serious. "I would."

"It's so far away," Amy stammered. "Please don't go, Lou. Stay here with us."

Lou straightened up, her blue eyes angry. "What would be the point?" she snapped. "You've made it perfectly clear that you don't want my help around here!"

Amy felt torn. She didn't want the changes that her sister was suggesting but she desperately wanted Lou to stay. "I do. I..."

"Give it a break, Amy!" Lou interrupted bitterly. "I know what you think. Don't try and pretend otherwise."

"But, Lou..."

"I don't want to talk about it!" Lou raised her voice. "And that's the end of the discussion!" Banging the buckets down on to the floor, she turned and walked out of the feed-room.

After Carl had eaten breakfast, he and Lou got ready to leave for the airport. "Thank you for having me to stay," Carl said, shaking hands with Grandpa. "It's been great." He turned to Amy and winked. "See you later."

"Bye," Amy said curtly. She wished he had never come. If it wasn't for him, Lou wouldn't be thinking about going away.

Lou tucked her arm through his. "Come on, we don't want to miss your plane." She turned to Grandpa. "I'll be back by lunchtime."

"Remember we're going to the cinema this afternoon," he told her.

Lou nodded.

"Pity I couldn't stay," Carl said. "But work calls."

Thank goodness! Amy thought to herself.

After Carl and Lou had driven off, Amy went to Spartan's stall. She had decided to take him out to graze again.

Spartan's eyes rolled angrily and he pawed the ground as she led him out of his stall. His ears were back, but Amy barely noticed. She couldn't stop thinking about Lou going to Chicago. Reaching the grass, lost in her own world, she forgot she was leading Spartan and loosened the lead-rope.

Moving like a striking snake, Spartan pulled backwards, half rearing as he jerked his head up and out of her reach. The rope slipped through Amy's hands, burning the skin as it went. She staggered back in surprise. "Spartan!" she gasped.

The horse swung round beside her, his heavy shoulder colliding with her and knocking her off balance. Amy felt herself falling and reached out too late. Her head crashed against a wooden fence post. Then she slid to the ground and lay there, dazed.

In front of her Spartan rose up on his hind legs, his dark eyes glistened and he shrieked savagely as his front legs thrashed out. Amy looked up and saw his flailing hooves above her. She screamed and closed her eyes.

"Stop it!" Jack Bartlett's voice shouted. Amy's eyes flew open. Red in the face and out of breath, her grandfather was grasping the end of the lead-rope, frantically trying to pull the horse away. Distracted from his target, Spartan shook his head wildly and turned his attention on Jack Bartlett. Amy scrambled to her feet and, ignoring the wave of dizziness that swept over her, flung herself at Spartan's head.

Spartan plunged backwards at the touch of her hands on his halter but she held on desperately. "Steady!" she cried. At last Spartan came to a stop and he stood snorting, his body trembling with rage as he stared at her.

"Amy!" Grandpa exclaimed. "Are you OK?"

Amy nodded, not taking her eyes off Spartan for a second. "I'll put him back in his stall," she said. Not waiting for permission, she led Spartan up the yard. Her legs felt weak with shock.

Quickly, she put him in his stall and slipped out just in time before his hooves crashed defiantly into the wooden door.

The next instant Grandpa was beside her, his arms wrapping tightly around her. "Oh, Amy!" he exclaimed. "I thought he was going to kill you."

In the warmth and safety of his arms, the adrenaline left her and Amy's knees gave way. Grandpa supported her and helped her to the house. Then he gently inspected her head. "You'll have a lump there in the morning but I think it should be OK." He took her hand, his blue eyes shadowed with fear and relief. "When I looked out of the window and saw him knock you over, it was my worst nightmare come true."

"Thank goodness you were watching," Amy said, a cold shiver running down her spine at the thought of what might have happened if Grandpa hadn't been there.

Jack Bartlett stroked her hair. "That horse is vicious, Amy. We have no option but to put him down."

Amy stared at him. "Grandpa! We can't give up on him."

"We have to," her grandpa said, and his voice was firmer than Amy had ever heard it. "A horse like Spartan will never be cured. I know it's hard to accept but he's just one of those horses that Heartland can't help. I'll call Scott in the morning." When Amy opened her mouth to argue, Grandpa wouldn't let her speak. "I'm sorry, but over this I am going to have my way." He squeezed her shoulder. "You are far more precious to me than any horse."

Amy's voice rose desperately. "But Grandpa..."

"No, Amy," Grandpa said sadly. "No buts. Not this time." He sighed. "Now I think you should go to bed and rest for a while."

Amy walked numbly up the stairs. Pulling off her jeans, she got into bed. She couldn't stand by and watch Spartan be put down. There just had to be something that he would respond to...

The answer came to her in a flash. *Join-up!* She hadn't tried it before because she had been worried that Spartan would try and jump out of the ring – but this was her last chance. By joining-up with him she might be able to win back his trust. Hope flickered through her. Spartan *might* try and escape but it was a risk she was prepared to take if there was the possibility that his life could be saved.

She sat up in bed. When could she do it? It had to be a time when no one was around. There was no way Grandpa was going to let her anywhere near Spartan again.

Just then there was a knock on her bedroom door and her grandpa came in. "How are you feeling?" he asked.

"My head still hurts a bit," Amy replied. "But I'm OK."

"Looks like we won't be going to the cinema this afternoon, then," Grandpa said.

The cinema! Amy had forgotten about the trip to see a film that afternoon. A plan formed in her mind. Putting a hand to her head, she lay back in bed. "Well, my head hurts too much to go, but there's no point you and Lou missing out," she said. "You could still make it. I'll be fine here."

Grandpa shook his head. "It's Ty's day off and I can't leave you on your own after a knock like that."

"I'll phone Matt. He can come and look after me," Amy said.

Grandpa didn't look convinced.

"It would be good for you and Lou to spend the time together," Amy said. "You could talk to her about going to Chicago. She'll probably open up more if I'm not there." Amy looked at Grandpa. "You don't want her to go, do you?"

"Of course I don't, but it's up to her." Grandpa seemed lost in thought for a moment. "It would be good to have a chance to talk to Lou, though." He stood up. "We'll see how you're feeling in a couple of hours."

By the afternoon, Amy had finally managed to convince Grandpa and Lou that she was quite happy to be left on her own. She'd given Matt a call. "I'll be fine," she said to Grandpa when he came up to her room after lunch. "I've rung Matt." She didn't add that Matt had been out playing soccer and that she'd told his mom that it wasn't important.

"OK, then," Grandpa said. "We won't be long. Promise me you'll rest."

"I promise," Amy said.

Grandpa frowned. "Maybe we should wait for Matt to arrive."

"No!" Amy said quickly. She saw his look of surprise. "If you don't leave now, you'll miss the start of the film."

"I guess you're right," Grandpa said reluctantly. He bent down and kissed her. "You take care."

Amy nodded and faked a yawn. "I think I might go to sleep for a little while."

Grandpa looked relieved. "Good girl. See you later, then."

Amy lay in her bed and listened to his footsteps going downstairs, then the sound of Grandpa and Lou getting into the car and the engine starting. She got out of bed, crept to the window and watched them driving off. *At last!*

She waited a few minutes to make sure they were safely gone, then pulled on her jeans and ran down the stairs and out of the house. It was quiet on the yard. The air felt heavy and still and the horses were barely shifting in their stalls. In the distance dark clouds were gathering. Amy felt sure a storm was brewing.

She fetched a long-line from the tack-room and with her heart thudding in her chest, she approached Spartan's stall. The quietness on the yard was so unusual that for a moment Amy felt a flicker of loneliness. She was completely on her own — alone with Spartan. She took a deep breath. It was the way it had to be.

She opened the stall door. Spartan leapt backwards, his muscles bunched under his bay coat, his neck high. Adrenaline coursing through her, Amy slipped inside. "Easy, boy," she said.

Spartan snorted, the sound loud in the still air. Talking all the while, Amy approached him. As the horse's hindquarters swung round Amy moved quickly, closing in on his head and taking hold of his halter before he could kick out. "Oh, Spartan," she said in desperation. "You don't need to be like this."

Taking another deep breath, Amy clipped the long-line to the halter and led him out. He pranced angrily beside her. A heavy drop of rain fell on Amy's arm and then another. She ignored them: rain or no rain she only had this one opportunity to work with Spartan. In a couple of hours Grandpa and Lou would be back and her chance would be gone.

She led Spartan into the ring, securing the gate behind

her. As she took him into the middle she looked anxiously at the fence. It wasn't high. Only just over a metre. He could clear it easily. Her fingers hesitated by the clip of the long-line. What if he escaped? But what choice did she have? With one swift move she unhooked the line. It was a risk she would just have to take. She stepped back.

Spartan jerked his head and stopped, a look of surprise on his face. Realizing that he was free, he let out a wild snort and tossed his head in the air, wheeling around on his back legs. Then to Amy's horror he set off straight towards the fence.

"Stop!" she shouted, running after him.

Spartan jerked to a halt, his front feet stamping into the sand. He spun round and looked at her. Amy stopped in her tracks. She was caught in the savage glare of his eyes. She realized that for the first time *ever* in her life she felt completely afraid of a horse. She was suddenly aware of how horribly vulnerable she was with only the long-line in her hand. She took an uncertain step backwards. There was a sudden roll of thunder, and with a screaming cry Spartan plunged towards her.

As he thundered over the sand Amy's fear suddenly disappeared, drowned in the wave of blind fury that swept over her. How *dare* he attack her! After she had defended him, cared for him, believed in him! With every bit of strength in her body she flung the long-line towards him. "*No!*" she shouted, almost incoherent with rage.

Startled by the flying rope, Spartan swerved and galloped past her. Amy grabbed the rope from the floor. "You can't blame me!" she screamed. "It wasn't my fault!" Stopping abruptly, Spartan turned and reared, his eyes gleaming with hate and fury. His front legs flailed in the air. Amy slashed the rope towards him again. "It wasn't my fault!" she screamed again as she advanced on him. "It wasn't my fault!"

With a sudden snort of alarm, Spartan came down and galloped away from her. There was a loud crash as a second clap of thunder burst overhead. The rain started to beat down with a new intensity. Amy barely noticed it. Picking up the rope, she flung it after Spartan. "Go on!" she shouted. "Go on! Get away!"

Wherever he went she followed with the rope. White-hot anger coursed through her. Overhead a jagged fork of lightning blazed down through the sky. Water streamed down Amy's face, furious tears mingling with the pouring rain. On and on Spartan galloped, his coat streaked with sweat and rain as she forced him on through the crashing of the storm.

She had no idea how long she drove him round the ring for. But after many, many circles the rage seemed to start leaving Spartan's eyes. Amy saw his gallop steady and his inside ear flicker towards her. A shock ran through her. *Join-up! The first signal!* His wild circles, his attempts to escape from her had led to the first stage of join-up. There was no doubting it – his inside ear was fixed on her, his gallop was slowing to a steady canter.

Gasping for breath and soaked to the skin, she acted instinctively. She squared her shoulders with his and saw his head and neck lower. She sent him round in the opposite direction, her eyes fixed on his.

More circles. She hardly noticed that the thunder had passed. She wasn't satisfied yet. His acceptance of her had to be absolute. And then it happened, he started to chew. Stretching his head down until his muzzle was almost on the ground, he trotted round, his mouth chewing at the air, his neck pulled long and low.

Amy took a step back and turned her body away, dropping her eyes to the ground. From the corner of her eye she could see Spartan stop. He looked at her. His ears pricked. There was a long pause. She heard him move and the back of her neck prickled but she forced herself to stay still, eyes averted. The breath gasped in her throat and her heart pounded. What if he decided to attack her again? He was close now, getting closer. She could hear his hooves thudding softly into the wet sand, hear his heavy breathing. Amy suddenly realized it had stopped raining.

Suddenly she felt warm breath on the back of her neck, a muzzle on her shoulder. Hardly daring to breathe, she slowly turned round. Spartan stood there. His sides were heaving, his coat was streaked with rain and sweat but the fire had left his eyes. Very gently, Amy reached out and rubbed his face. For the first time since coming to Heartland, Spartan accepted her touch.

Amy felt her eyes filling with tears. Tears of relief and joy washing away the weeks of unrelenting guilt. "Spartan," she whispered. She caught the sob that rose in her throat. "It wasn't my fault," she whispered, leaning her head against his wet neck and hearing his laboured breathing. "It really wasn't my fault."

As the tears on her face merged with the sweat on his neck she suddenly knew that it was true — she wasn't to blame for the accident. As Grandpa had said, Mom would never have gone out that night if she hadn't wanted to. Fresh tears sprang to Amy's eyes, tears that welled from the very depth of her heart — tears of grief and loss, no longer held back by the crushing weight of guilt. Wrapping her arms around Spartan's neck she sobbed into his mane, releasing the tears that she had been unable to shed at the cemetery.

At long last her sobs quietened and Spartan's breathing slowed. Amy drew back and realized that the clouds were parting. The sun shone through, causing the leaves on the trees surrounding the schooling ring to shimmer and glow.

A new determination filled her, hot and fierce. She might not be able to bring her mom back but she *could* help Spartan. She kissed him. "I promise I'll make you happy, Spartan," she whispered as he turned and focused on her. "I promise." As she looked into his dark eyes, she knew that her mom would have approved.

Amy slowly led Spartan back down to his stall where she

fetched a hay net and rubbed him down. As she swept the cloth over his back she suddenly paused. Just by his withers he seemed to have a patch of white hairs coming through. It was the first time she had ever been close enough to see. She examined the area closely, parting the hair with her fingers. Her eyes widened. It was an old freeze-mark. The fur over the freeze-mark had been dyed brown to match his coat but now the white hair was growing back through. The people who had stolen him must have done it so that he couldn't be traced. She looked more closely. It was impossible to read the letters with the two colours of hair but maybe if the area was clipped the letters would become more visible. Excitement surged through Amy. Maybe Spartan's old owners could be traced. Maybe he could be reunited with them and lead a normal life again.

She finished rubbing him down and then sank down on some straw by the manger. Spartan was pulling happily at the sweet-smelling hay. Amy watched him, marvelling at the change in his eyes and demeanour. Relaxed and peaceful, he munched on his hay, occasionally swishing his tail.

He could do with a good groom, Amy thought, but then she yawned, too exhausted to move. She could do it later. Leaning her head back, she closed her eyes. Just two minutes' rest, she thought. Her eyelashes flickered on her cheeks, and within seconds she was fast asleep.

Chapter Seven

"Amy! Oh my God!"

Amy woke up with a jump at the sound of Lou's voice. Confused, she blinked and looked up.

Lou was staring down at her, her face pale. "Grandpa! Quick!" she shouted over her shoulder. "Something's happened to Amy!"

"No, I'm OK," Amy said hastily, scrambling to her feet. "I was just asleep."

Jack Bartlett came hurrying up to the door. "What on earth are you doing in there?" he demanded.

Amy saw the fear on his face. "I'm OK," she repeated. She hastened to explain. "Spartan's better." She moved towards the horse.

"Amy! Come out of there at once," Lou said, her voice high.

"No. Look!" Amy put her hand gently on Spartan's shoulder, hoping he would respond positively – that the join-up really had been a success. He turned his head enquiringly. Amy was relieved to see that his eyes were calm. She moved round to the front of him and rubbed his forehead. "See," she said, turning to Grandpa and Lou who were watching open-mouthed.

"What's happened to him?" Lou gasped.

"I joined-up with him and now he trusts me." As she spoke, Amy realized how inadequate the words seemed. She could never fully convey the experience she remembered – the explosion of fury and guilt, the anger, the savageness. All mirrored in the violent storm that had reminded her of the night of the accident. She had never experienced anything like it and, amazing though it had been, she hoped never to have to go through anything like it again.

Lou and Grandpa looked disbelieving but the evidence was there for them to see. Spartan stood as gentle as little Sugarfoot as Amy stroked him.

Grandpa opened the stall door. "Amy Fleming," he said, running a despairing hand through his hair, "I didn't want you ever to go near Spartan again."

"I know," Amy said. She grinned at him. "But isn't it lucky I did?" She came out of the stall. "You know Mom would have done the same, Grandpa."

Jack Bartlett looked at her for a moment and then swept her into his arms. "Yes, honey," he said, kissing her hair. "I know she would."

* * *

Amy called Scott to let him know about her breakthrough and about the freeze-mark she had found on Spartan's back. And then, for the first time in ages, she slept peacefully through the night.

Amy got up early the next morning. The sun was shining in through her window. She pulled on her clothes and went outside.

Behind Heartland the trees on the ridges of the hills stood out dark green against the pale blue of the sky. Amy looked around, breathing in deeply and enjoying the cool of the morning air. She felt wonderfully refreshed and determined in her resolve to do everything she could to help Spartan.

As soon as Ty arrived she filled him in on the events of the day before and took him to see Spartan.

"I thought if we clipped the hair then the freeze-mark might show through more clearly," she said.

"I'll get the clippers," Ty agreed. When he came back Spartan was nuzzling at Amy's shoulder. He shook his head. "I'm going to take days off more often!" he joked. "He's a different horse."

Amy patted Spartan. "He's not. He's just become the horse he was, again."

"Because of you," Ty said. "You believed in him, Amy. You made the change in him possible."

Amy felt her cheeks go pink.

Spartan moved beside them. "Well ... I guess we'd better get on with this clipping," Ty said, his voice suddenly brisk.

Amy moved automatically round to Spartan's head. "Easy now," she murmured to the horse as Ty switched the clippers on. Spartan flinched but settled as Amy stroked him.

It only took a minute. "All done," Ty said, turning the clippers off.

Amy looked eagerly at the rectangle of clipped hair. Six white numbers stood out clearly against Spartan's bay coat.

Ty pulled a pen out of his pocket and a piece of paper. He scribbled down the numbers. "Now all we need to do is ring the freeze-marking centre."

"I wonder what Spartan's owners are like," Amy said.

"I guess we'll find out soon enough," Ty said.

Amy took the piece of paper with the number on it and went down to the house to use the phone in the kitchen. She rang the freeze-marking centre and they explained how they would try and trace Spartan's owner. "Although," they warned her, "sometimes the details we have of the owners are out of date or wrong if the horse has been sold and our records not updated."

As Amy put the phone down she realized Lou had been listening to the conversation.

"I hope they're successful," Lou said. "Especially now you've cured him."

"*Started* curing him," Amy corrected her. She knew that Spartan wasn't fully better yet: he needed to build up his confidence with everyone, not just her. She was about to cut the conversation and then hesitated. All their disagreements suddenly seemed so pointless. "What are you doing?"

"Just running through the list of things that I still have to organize for this dance," Lou replied.

"Is there anything I can do to help?" Amy asked.

Lou looked up, her blue eyes showing her surprise. "You think the whole thing's a stupid idea," she said. "Why would you want to help?"

Amy's cheeks flushed. "I don't think it's stupid. Well, maybe I did at first," she admitted, seeing Lou's expression. "But people do seem interested in coming. I ... I hope it works." She smiled at Lou, suddenly aware that she really meant it.

Amy spent the next few hours bonding further with Spartan. She took him out in the circular ring and joined-up with him again, then spent ages grooming him, trying to brush out the scurf and grease that had built up in his coat over the last few weeks. Finally she massaged dilute lavender oil into his nostrils to help soothe and relax him.

Ty looked over the door as she was finishing. "Lavender," he said, sniffing the air. "That should help with his nervousness."

Amy nodded. "Can you think of anything else that might be good for him? Although he trusts me now, I want something to help him get over the mental trauma of the past couple of months."

"I'd give him some walnut flower remedy," Ty said. "Your mom used to use that on horses that needed help adjusting to new circumstances – and how about giving him a table-spoon of honey in his feed?"

"Oh, yes," Amy said, pleased with the idea. She knew that honey was excellent for channelling energy. Her mom had found that it seemed to make certain difficult horses more manageable: it energized them at the same time as making them willing to please.

Just then there was a sound of a car coming up the drive. "It's Matt and Scott," Ty said.

Amy came out of the stall.

"Hi!" she called as the car came to a halt and Matt and Scott jumped out.

"Hi, Amy," Scott called. "Hi, Ty."

"Hey there." Ty greeted him warmly. He was good friends with the vet.

"Great news about Spartan!" Matt said to Amy as they reached the stall. "Scott told me. You must be really pleased."

"Spartan's like a different horse," Ty said. "See how he is with Amy now."

Scott watched as Amy went into the stall and touched Spartan all over. "You've had a real breakthrough," he said. "Well done!"

Amy's eyes sparkled and she came over to the door. "It was all through joining-up with him. I don't know why I didn't try it sooner."

"Have you heard any news from the freeze-mark centre or from Spartan's owner?" Scott asked.

"None yet," Amy replied.

"Bet you can't wait till they ring," Matt said. "Then Spartan can go back to his real home."

"I guess," Amy said. She tried to sound more positive. "Yeah. It will be good."

"But it will be hard to say goodbye to him, huh?" Scott said, looking sympathetically at her.

Amy nodded and caught Ty's eye. "Very."

"So you *don't* want him to go?" Matt said, sounding confused. "I thought you wanted his owners to get in touch."

"I did ... I do," Amy said. She saw the confusion on Matt's face. It was obvious he didn't understand. She sighed, wishing, not for the first time, that Matt understood about horses in the way Scott and Ty did. Maybe then imagining him as a boyfriend wouldn't be so hard.

After lunch, as Amy came out of the house she heard a low whinny. She looked at the front stable block, expecting to see Pegasus's head over his stall door. It wasn't Pegasus, though, it was Spartan. He whickered again. Amy smiled. "Hi there, boy." She walked over and stroked his face.

As she stroked him, she thought about how she was going to rehabilitate him. Amy knew it wasn't enough for him simply to trust her – he had to learn to have confidence in other people as well. She would have to get as many people as possible to handle him — Grandpa, Lou, Ty, and Scott when he called by.

She smoothed his long forelock. And what about riding him? A thrill ran through her at the thought. When should she try that? She decided to ask Ty what he thought.

She found him filling the evening hay nets from the small stock of hay in the feed-room. "Hi there," he said, looking up as she came in.

"I was thinking," Amy blurted out her question, "when do you think I should try riding Spartan?" She felt the breath catch in her throat. What would Ty say? She respected his opinion and knew that, much as she wanted to ride Spartan, if Ty told her to wait a month then she would.

Ty shrugged. "The end of the week?" he suggested.

"That soon?" Amy said.

"Sure," Ty nodded. "If he continues to improve then why put it off? It should help his confidence. You'll be able to take him out and let him have new experiences."

Excitement flooded through Amy. The end of the week! She couldn't wait!

Over the next few days, Amy spent as much time as she could with Spartan, handling him, grooming him, lunging him and getting other people to come into his stall and handle him too. Gradually the lingering nervousness started to leave his eyes. However, a certain reserve seemed to remain. Amy puzzled over it. Spartan was affectionate and his confidence seemed to grow every day but it was as if he was holding something back. She wondered whether she was imagining it — she didn't mention it to anyone and no one else, not even Ty, seemed to notice.

On Friday morning, she was grooming Spartan when Ty looked over the door. "Have you thought any more about riding him?" he asked.

"Yeah, loads," Amy said. "I can't wait to try."

"So why don't you try today?" Ty said.

"Today?" Amy said, her heart leaping with excitement. "You think he's ready?"

"Yes," Ty replied. "Do you want me to fetch a saddle and bridle?"

Amy nodded eagerly. Her fingers trembled with anticipation as she quickly finished off grooming the horse. Thoughts whirled through her brain. She was going to ride Spartan! What would he be like? She stroked his broad back and imagined sitting on him. He looked fantastic to ride. Her heart raced as she remembered that she knew nothing about his history. He might not even have been ridden before. He might throw her off. She ran her fingers through Spartan's mane and kissed his neck. She didn't care. She just wanted to give it a go.

When Ty returned with the tack, Spartan sniffed at the bridle curiously but didn't seem to object when Amy took it and slipped it on over his head.

"Now for the saddle," she said, trying to keep her voice

calm, although inside her stomach was fluttering nervously. Spartan's reaction to the saddle would give them a good indication if he had been ridden before. He stood still as she placed the saddle on his back and did up the girth.

"So far so good," Ty said, glancing at her. "He wouldn't be this calm if he hadn't been backed."

Amy nodded in relief. "Now I've just got to get on."

"I'd lunge him first," Ty said. "Just to get him used to moving with the saddle and bridle on and give him a chance to get rid of any excess energy."

They led Spartan up to the training ring and Amy started to lunge him. Spartan bucked once as he first moved into a trot but then settled down into a steady rhythm. After five minutes, Amy brought him to a halt and looked at Ty.

"Here goes," she said, pulling the stirrups down.

Ty moved to Spartan's head and held the reins while Amy mounted. She felt Spartan move nervously as she sank lightly down into the saddle but she patted his neck and soothed him and he quickly settled.

Amy picked up his reins and gently squeezed with her legs. Spartan walked forward. He felt calm and relaxed, and after a few circuits round the ring Amy started to relax too. She shortened her reins and squeezed him into a trot. With his long stride he seemed to float across the sand.

"He feels wonderful!" she gasped to Ty.

Amy asked Spartan to canter and he made the transition smoothly. She cantered three circles, grinning in delight.

Spartan was every bit as fantastic to ride as she had imagined.

At last she drew him to a halt. "Wow!" she gasped, patting his warm bay neck and smiling at Ty in delight. "He's gorgeous!"

"He looked great," Ty said.

Amy took her feet out of the stirrups and dismounted. "I'd better make that do for today," she said.

"Something tells me you'll be riding him again tomorrow," Ty said with a grin.

"I think you might be right," she smiled back.

Ty opened the gate and Amy led Spartan down the yard. Just as she finished untacking him, the phone rang. Leaving the tack outside the stall, Amy ran to the house. She reached the phone just before Lou, who had come in from collecting vegetables from the back garden.

"Heartland," Amy said breathlessly. "Amy Fleming speaking."

"Hi." The man's voice was deep. "My name's Larry Boswell. I've been contacted by the freeze-mark centre. I believe you have a horse of mine – a bay with a white star. He was stolen."

It was Spartan's owner!

"Hello ... are you there?" the man said.

"Yes ... yes, I am," Amy said quickly.

"And do you have my horse?" the man said.

"Yes," Amy said, her stomach seeming to flip over. "We do."

Chapter Eight

"That's fantastic news!" Larry Boswell said. "I can't believe you found him!" Amy could hear the emotion in his voice. "I never thought I'd see him again. He was stolen three months ago. How long have you had him?"

"Almost two weeks," Amy said. "But he was at the vet's for six weeks before that."

"The vet's?"

Amy explained about the accident and Larry Boswell listened intently. When she had finished he whistled. "That's awful. I'm really sorry to hear about your mom. I can't thank you enough for taking Gerry in after all you've been through."

"Gerry?" Amy echoed.

"That's his name. Short for Geronimo. Full name Dancing Grass Geronimo," Larry Boswell told her. "He's one of my

89

best stallions. I have a stud farm, you see – I breed Morgans. Now, when would it be suitable for me to come over and collect him – my farm's about two hours away?"

Fetch him. Amy's mouth felt suddenly dry. "Well ... er ... whenever you like," she stammered. After all she had been through with Spartan the thought of losing him was hard to believe. *But you wanted to find his owners,* she reminded herself. *You wanted Spartan to be happy.*

"Great!" said Larry Boswell. "I'll be over this afternoon, about three o'clock. Can you give me some directions?"

By the time she put the phone down, Amy was feeling stunned. For a moment she was unable to move.

"What's wrong?" Lou asked.

"Spartan's owner is coming to collect him today."

"But that's great!" Lou exclaimed. She saw Amy's face and frowned uncertainly. "Isn't it?"

Tears prickled at the back of Amy's eyes. She nodded.

"You're going to miss him, aren't you?" Lou said softly.

Amy swallowed.

Lou put her arm around her. "It's the right thing to happen, Amy. He couldn't stay here. At least this way he'll go to people he knows and who love him."

Amy knew Lou was right. Horses came to Heartland with the aim of being healed so that they could go to new homes or back to their owners. It was a rule their mom had insisted upon and that Amy had grown up with. But somehow with Spartan it was different.

"I don't want him to go," she whispered.

"I know you don't," Lou said, hugging her. "But it's for the best. You know it is. We can't keep him here if he has the chance of a happy life with someone else."

Amy fought back her tears and nodded reluctantly.

From two-thirty onwards Amy waited in the kitchen with Lou and Ty, watching the driveway.

"What did he sound like?" Ty asked Amy.

"OK, I guess," she replied, pacing up and down.

"It'll be fine," Lou said. "You'll see. Stop worrying." She looked down the drive. "Here's Scott."

Amy had been in touch with the vet soon after speaking to Larry Boswell to tell him the news.

Scott parked his car and came into the house. "Not here yet?"

Amy shook her head.

Ten minutes later, a pick-up pulling a trailer came up the drive. "It's him!" Amy exclaimed, her stomach turning with anticipation.

The pick-up stopped. A short, thick-set man with grey hair got out. "Hi," he said, as they came out of the farmhouse to meet him. "I'm Larry Boswell."

Lou took charge of the situation and introduced everyone. Larry Boswell shook hands. "I can't tell you how pleased I am." He looked at Amy. "Like I said on the telephone, I own a stud farm – but Gerry, he's always been real special to me. I hand-reared him as a foal." His eyes scanned the stalls eagerly. "Where is he?"

Amy swallowed. "I'll get him," she said.

Spartan was tied up in his stall. As Amy entered, he pricked his ears and nickered a welcome. Amy thought he looked beautiful. He still had his scars – they would stay with him for ever – but his bay coat gleamed, his tail hung soft and silky below his hocks, and the star on his forehead stood out, snowy-white. "Oh, Spartan," she whispered, her heart aching. "It's time to say goodbye."

As she untied the rope he nuzzled affectionately against her. Giving him a kiss, Amy led him out of the stall.

Larry Boswell was looking around eagerly. "Gerry!" he exclaimed as soon as he saw him.

Spartan stopped dead at the sound of Larry Boswell's voice. His head flew up. His ears pricked. A shrill whinny burst from him and he plunged in the direction of Larry Boswell, pulling the lead-rope clean out of Amy's hands. The horse trotted over and stopped in front of his owner.

"Oh, Gerry, Gerry," Larry Boswell murmured, stroking the horse's ears, neck and face. "I never thought I'd see you again."

Amy stood, astonished, rooted to the spot where Spartan had left her. She watched as the horse nuzzled Larry Boswell ecstatically. There was no mistaking the love in his eyes – in either of their eyes.

Larry Boswell gently examined the scars along Spartan's

side. "You're not going to be winning much in the show-ring from now on, are you, Gerry?" he said ruefully, patting the horse. "We'll have to leave winning those ribbons to your foals."

"Foals?" Amy said, eagerly stepping forward. "He's got foals?"

"Not yet," Larry Boswell said. "I'd just used him for conformation classes until he was stolen. But I'll put him to stud when I get him home. He should breed some good stock."

Amy's eyes widened. Larry Boswell obviously hadn't realized that Spartan had been gelded. "Um…" she said, glancing quickly at Scott for support. "You won't be able to use him for breeding."

Larry Boswell frowned. "Why not?"

Scott stepped forward. "He's been gelded, I'm afraid."

"What?" Larry Boswell replied in genuine astonishment.

Scott nodded. "It's the policy here at Heartland. Until last week there was no way of seeing his freeze-mark or even knowing for sure that he had been stolen. It was assumed that he would be re-homed, so he had to be gelded."

"This can't be true!" Mr Boswell exclaimed incredulously. "This horse is —" he corrected himself — "*was* a valuable breeding animal." He glared at Amy. "How could you do this? He was my most valuable stallion."

"We had no idea," Amy stammered, taken aback by his sudden anger.

Larry Boswell's voice rose. "He's got some of the best blood-lines in my stock. Each of his foals would have fetched thousands of dollars!"

"I'm sorry," Amy said, feeling close to tears. "I really am, I…"

"You'll be hearing from my lawyers about this!" Larry Boswell shouted.

Lou stepped forward. "Now, Mr Boswell, please…"

The man ignored her. Letting go of Spartan, he pushed past Amy and Lou and headed towards his car. Ty grabbed Spartan as he tried to follow him.

"Mr Boswell…" Lou cried. "What about your horse?"

"This horse here doesn't resemble any horse that I know!" Larry Boswell shouted.

Scott stepped out in front of the angry man. "I think you should consider carefully what you are saying, Mr Boswell," he said, his voice calm but full of authority. Mr Boswell pulled up short. There was no way he could push Scott's tall, broad-shouldered frame out of the way. "Amy and her family took in your horse," Scott continued, looking round at Amy and Lou. "Despite their own tragic loss, they looked after him and made every effort to trace you. In my opinion you should be thanking them, not threatening legal action."

"Yes… but…" Larry Boswell blustered, his face flushing a deep red.

"Thanks to them you still have a horse," Scott said firmly. "Believe me, Mr Boswell, you have *every* reason to be grateful."

For a moment, Larry Boswell looked as if he was going to argue further but then his shoulders suddenly seemed to sag. "You're right," he muttered.

Amy felt the breath leave her in a rush. She met Lou's eye and saw her relief.

Larry Boswell shook his head. "I guess you did what you had to, and I appreciate all the heartbreak that you've been through on his behalf." He glanced at Spartan. "But Gerry being gelded changes everything."

Amy was astonished. "Why?"

Larry Boswell shrugged. "What use would he be? I have a business to run. I can't have a horse that won't pay his way."

Amy couldn't believe what she was hearing. "You can't just leave him here!" she exclaimed.

"Well, I'm not going to take him back with me," Larry Boswell said. "I'll pay your expenses for keeping him until you find him a new home – that's the best I can offer."

Amy looked at Spartan who was now shaking his head, trying to pull away from Ty. Spartan loved his master – that was completely clear. Although she didn't want to say goodbye to him, she knew that he belonged with Larry Boswell.

She stepped towards him. "Take Spartan with you," she pleaded.

Larry Boswell shook his head. "Sorry, young lady. That's the way it has to be." He walked slowly towards Spartan. "You know the rules, Gerry," he said softly. "I can't break them, not even for you." He reached up and gently stroked the horse's forehead. "No, not even for you." He turned to Amy. "I'll send you the ownership papers," he said. "Bill me for the livery charges." Then, squaring his shoulders, he strode back to his car.

As he drove away Spartan let out a high-pitched whinny and pulled forward. "Easy, boy," Ty said hastily.

Amy looked at the distress on Spartan's face and had to fight back the tears welling up in her eyes. She couldn't suppress a feeling of hatred for Larry Boswell. How could he do this to Spartan?

"Don't worry," Lou said calmly, her expression full of sympathy. "We'll find another home for him. You'll see."

"But he wants to be with his owner!" Amy cried.

"No, Lou's right, Amy," Scott said quickly. "There'll be other people who want to give him a home. He's a fine horse."

Ty nodded in agreement and clicked his tongue. "Come on, fella, let's put you back in your stall."

Lou looked gratefully at Scott as they followed Spartan up the yard. "Thanks for standing up for us to Mr Boswell. I don't know what we'd have done if he had gone ahead and sued."

"He wouldn't have got anywhere," Scott said.

"Thanks anyway," Lou said. She patted Spartan's back as he went into his stall. "I'm just glad he's getting better." She turned to Scott. "I wanted to ask you about Sugarfoot.

Would it be OK to put him out to graze in the field now? I've been cutting him fresh grass each day but it's not really the same."

"Turning him out for a few hours each day should be fine," Scott said. "As long as the weather's good, of course. I'll just give him a quick check over."

Scott fetched his bag from the car and then went up to Sugarfoot's stall with Amy and Lou. The pony was happily nibbling on the remains of grass that Lou had cut for him at lunchtime.

"How are you doing, boy?" Scott said to him, patting the Shetland's neck. He listened to Sugarfoot's heart and checked his breathing. "He's making fine progress," he said to Lou.

"Do you hear that, Sugarfoot? You're ready to go out in the paddock," Lou said. She turned to Amy. "Shall we take him up there now? It's such a nice day."

"That would be great," Amy said, her heart lifting a little.

Lou put on Sugarfoot's halter and then led the Shetland out to the turn-out field just behind the back barn. The grass was lush, rich with clover and dotted randomly with bright yellow buttercups. Sugarfoot's small ears pricked eagerly.

Amy opened the gate. The little pony trotted into the field, put his head down and snorted.

"Look at him!" Lou said.

Suddenly Sugarfoot sank down on to his knees and rolled, sending two white butterflies fluttering up into the air. He jumped to his feet, shook his head, and then plunged it into the sweet grass and started to graze.

Lou smiled. "Isn't it incredible to see him like this?"

Amy nodded. She could vividly remember the shock of seeing Sugarfoot only a couple of weeks ago. Then he had been lying in his stall, breathing faintly, too weak to stand, half starved but too unhappy to eat. Now here he was, grazing happily in the field. "It's so wonderful that he's better," she said.

"I know," Lou agreed, her eyes glowing. "I can't believe the change in him. You know, I don't think there's anything better than seeing a sick animal recover. It's just such a good feeling!"

"I second that," Scott said softly.

"So it's better than clinching a deal at the bank?" Amy teased her, as they started walking back to the house.

"You bet!" Lou said. "A million times better!"

Amy was surprised to see a metallic black sports car with flashy alloy wheels parked outside the farmhouse. The driver's door swung open as they approached.

"Carl!" Lou gasped. "What are you doing here?"

Chapter Nine

Carl stepped out of the car. "Well, *that's* a nice greeting," he said.

Lou hurried forward. "You weren't supposed to be coming until tomorrow!"

"I took the day off." Carl put his arms around her. "I couldn't bear to be away from you another minute."

Lou pulled back. "Carl, this is Scott Trewin," she said, looking from one to the other, "our local vet. Scott, this is Carl Anderson."

Carl offered his hand to Scott. "Pleased to meet you."

Scott shook his hand. "Likewise," he said, but Amy noticed that his voice was cool. He turned to her. "I'd better go. I've got clients to see."

"Sure. Thanks for coming," she replied.

"Bye, Scott!" Lou called after him.

Scott drove off in a cloud of exhaust fumes with the doors of his Chevy rattling as usual.

Carl raised his eyebrows. "Can't he afford to drive anything better than that heap of junk?"

Before Amy could say anything, Lou had leapt to Scott's defence. "Scott's a brilliant vet!" she said hotly. "He spends all his money reinvesting in his veterinary practice, not spending it on fancy cars!"

Amy looked at her sister in surprise. It wasn't like Lou to sound so intense.

As they went into the house, Lou started to tell Carl about Sugarfoot. "He's so much better," she said. "We just turned him out in the paddock and it was wonderful, he looked so happy!"

"Great," Carl said, sounding rather bored. He dumped his bag on the floor. "Any chance of a drink?"

Amy saw Lou's face fall in disappointment. He wasn't showing any interest in what she was telling him. "Yeah, sure," Lou said flatly and headed for the fridge.

Leaving Lou and Carl in the house, Amy went back outside. She was sweeping the yard in front of the stable block and thinking about what they could do to find Spartan a home, when Lou and Carl came out. The horses were all looking out over their stall doors. Lou walked over to Spartan and offered him a mint. But the bay horse ignored her as he stared down the drive, his ears pricked, his head up.

Lou stroked his neck. "Poor thing," she murmured. "Don't worry, we'll find you another home soon."

Carl frowned. "With those scars?" he said. "I doubt it!"

Amy stopped brushing and glared at him. "Not everyone cares just about appearance!" she snapped.

Carl frowned in genuine astonishment. "You mean there are actually people who wouldn't mind?"

"Of course there are!" Amy said hotly.

Lou stepped in hastily. "I guess the most important thing is that we find him the *right* home." She turned and began to walk along the row of horses, feeding them all mints.

Carl followed her. "So, how about Chicago?" he said, putting put his arm round her. "Have you decided yet?"

Amy looked up. To her relief she saw that Lou was shaking her head. "No, not yet."

"I don't understand what the problem is," Carl said.

"It's a big decision to make, Carl," Lou replied. "If I do come I'll be leaving everything here."

"Oh, come on, Lou," Carl said. "You can't seriously want to go on playing the country girl forever."

"Why not?" Lou said rather crossly.

"You love the city — you're great there," Carl replied.

"Don't try and tell me what I am!" Lou said.

Carl immediately backed off. "I'm sorry."

"Good," Lou said sharply. "Because I'm not going to be pressurized into anything. Coming to Chicago is a decision I have to make on my own."

"I understand," Carl said. "You know I do, and I'd never interfere. I respect you far too much for that."

Lou looked slightly mollified and didn't seem to object when Carl slipped his arm around her shoulder again. "It's only because I want you to be with me so much," he said in a soft voice.

Amy had heard enough. She hurried away up the yard.

The next morning, Amy rode Spartan again. He was just as good in the training ring as he had been the day before so she decided to take him out of the yard.

Spartan jogged excitedly as they rode along the track behind Heartland and up the hillside. It was a warm day and Amy chose a shady trail. The sun slanted down between the canopy of leaves, casting shadows on the sandy ground. Spartan pricked his ears as he stepped among the trees. Amy could feel him start to tense up. She patted him and he jumped. "What's the matter?" she said. "It's OK."

Spartan walked cautiously on, his nostrils blowing, his neck outstretched. As they rounded the corner the trees thickened, blocking out the sun overhead. Spartan stopped and stared. Amy felt her stomach turn. *A canopy of trees.* A tidal wave of emotion overwhelmed her as memories of the night of the storm flooded back.

Spartan sensed her fear and stepped backwards, his hoof landing on a dry branch which broke with a resounding crack. With a terrified snort, Spartan reared high into the air.

"Spartan!" Amy gasped, throwing herself forward just in time. Spartan's front legs thrashed out, his eyes wide with fear. He landed on all four feet but in an instant was up in the air again, higher this time, so high that he seemed on the point of crashing over backwards. Losing her stirrup, Amy let go of the reins and hung on to his mane. He stayed balanced there for what seemed like an eternity to Amy and then came down and set off at a wild gallop along the track.

Amy clutched his mane desperately, grabbing for the reins, trying to get her stirrup back. "Spartan! Whoa!" she cried. But by now the horse was in a blind panic. He swerved round a corner and into a clearing.

Amy lurched in the saddle but the movement simultaneously swung the reins towards her. She grabbed them and then, throwing her weight back, pulled hard. "Steady! Steady, boy!"

Spartan came to a halt, his sides heaving and his neck damp with sweat. Amy stroked him. Her hands were trembling. What had she just done? In one unthinking moment had she wrecked all her good work with Spartan? She glanced back at the tunnel of trees. Suddenly she was gripped with Spartan's fear. She wanted to get away, as far away as possible from the memory of that awful night.

Be calm. Amy suddenly heard her mom's voice clear in her mind. *Be the horse's strength*, the voice whispered. *Control your own fear.*

Amy took a deep breath. Her hands stopped shaking.

"Silly boy," she said to Spartan, her voice normal apart from a slight tremor. "What was all that about?"

Spartan's ears flickered. It took immense resolve, but Amy knew what she had to do. She shortened her reins and turned him towards the trees. "You mustn't be scared," she said. "Nothing's going to happen to you."

She knew that Spartan didn't understand her words but she hoped that her tone of voice and firm leg-aids would reassure him. She also knew that she had to get him back through the tunnel of trees, otherwise his fear would grow and grow. "Walk on," she commanded.

Spartan hesitated.

"Walk on!" Amy said more firmly.

This time Spartan did as he was told. He took a step forward and then another. Forcing down her own fear, Amy patted his neck as he walked cautiously through the canopy of trees. "Good boy!" she praised, patting him.

At last they were out on the other side. It was then, and only then, that Amy allowed herself to dismount. She leant against Spartan, her legs feeling weak with relief. She had done it – got him through. He nuzzled her, his eyes calm again.

"Oh, Spartan," she said, patting him. He put his head down to graze. Amy sighed. No matter how much he had come on, there was such a long way to go before he would be ready to be re-homed. And then they had to find someone who would fully understand him.

She picked up the reins. "Come on, boy," she said, shaking her head. "Let's go home."

As she rode into the yard, Ty was coming out of Pegasus's stall. "How was he?" he asked.

"Not so good," Amy replied. She was about to explain what had happened when the kitchen door opened and Lou came hurrying out.

"Amy!" She looked very excited. "I'm so glad you're back!"

"Why? What's the matter?" Amy said.

"The most amazing thing has just happened!" Lou said. "I've just had a phone call from a man looking for a horse for his thirteen-year-old daughter. She sounds absolutely ideal!"

"Ideal for what?" Amy said in confusion.

Lou's eyes glowed. "For *Spartan*, of course! They'd read about us in a magazine and were delighted when I said we had a horse ready for re-homing!"

Amy stared at Lou. "You're not serious?"

"But they sounded perfect." Lou looked at her in confusion. "I thought you'd be pleased. I thought you wanted to find Spartan a good home."

"Not yet!" Amy exclaimed. "He's nowhere near ready to go. You'll just have to ring them back and tell them that he's not available."

"They'll have already left. I told them they could come and see him right away. I thought it would be fine. They're even bringing their trailer."

"Lou!" Amy cried incredulously. "How could you? Why didn't you check with me first?"

Lou looked like she didn't know what to say. "I'm ... I'm sorry," she stammered. "But you weren't here – I thought you'd be pleased."

"That's great!" Amy said. "Just great!" She shook her head. "Well, they can't have him. *You* can tell them that when they arrive!" Grabbing Spartan's reins she marched into his stall.

"Amy! Hang on!" Ty said, following her.

"What?" Amy said.

"Maybe it's not such a bad thing after all. OK, I agree with you that Spartan's not ready to go just now, but if they are the right family for him they won't mind waiting for him to be ready."

Amy frowned at him. "You mean, you think I should let them see Spartan?"

"Definitely," Ty said.

Spartan nuzzled against Amy's hand. She patted him. "He needs a really special home," she said quietly.

"I agree – but maybe this will be the one," Ty said.

Amy had a gut feeling that it wouldn't be, but she relented. "OK," she said. "I guess they can have a look at him."

The more Amy heard about the Satchwells from Lou, the more her reservations grew.

"Mr Satchwell said that Melanie, his daughter, has been

riding for three years," Lou explained as they waited for them to arrive after lunch. "She's just outgrown her old pony and they want a horse that she can take to the local pony club."

"Sounds ideal," said Carl, who was waiting with them.

"They don't sound very experienced," Amy objected. "Where would they keep him?"

"At their local livery stable and riding school."

"That would be all wrong for Spartan!" Amy exclaimed. "He needs a quiet home!"

"Amy, stay calm – just give them a chance," Ty said in a reassuring voice.

Just then, a gleaming white BMW pulling a top-of-the-range trailer came slowly up the driveway. The Satchwells got out.

"Max Satchwell," the father said, striding over towards Lou with his hand outstretched. "Pleased to meet you."

Lou introduced herself, Amy, Carl and Ty.

"I'm Nancy," said Mrs Satchwell, stepping gingerly over the gravel in her red open-toed sandals. "And this is Melanie, our daughter."

Amy looked Melanie Satchwell up and down. She was younger than Amy, dressed in spotless breeches and long, black riding boots. She had tightly curled red hair. "Hi," she said brightly to Amy. "I read about you in a magazine. My friends couldn't believe it when I said I was coming here! They were *so* jealous!"

"Ever since she saw the article, Melanie's been wanting a horse from here," Max Satchwell said, smiling fondly at his daughter. "Haven't you, pumpkin?"

Melanie ignored her father and looked round impatiently. "Can I see the horse?" she said eagerly.

"He's over there," Amy said, pointing to where Spartan was looking out over his stall door.

"The bay with the star?" Melanie said. Amy nodded. "Wow! He's gorgeous!" Before Amy could stop her Melanie had started running towards Spartan's door. Spartan snorted in alarm and shot backwards into his stall. "What did he do that for?" Melanie exclaimed, stopping dead and looking surprised.

"Because you were running!" Amy exclaimed. "He's a rescue horse! He's nervous."

Melanie looked embarrassed. "I'm sorry – Piper doesn't mind me running. He isn't nervous of anything."

"Well, Spartan is," Amy said sharply. "He's been through a lot."

Melanie looked over the door. "Look at his scars," she said. For a moment Amy wondered if it would stop her wanting him, but her hopes were dashed – Melanie turned round with a determined look on her face. "I want him, Daddy."

Max Satchwell got out his cheque book. He grinned at Lou. "Melanie always knows what she wants," he said. "Lucky we brought the trailer with us, hey? Now, you told me that you ask for a donation to Heartland. What sort of figure are we talking about?"

Amy couldn't stand it any longer. If Lou wouldn't say anything then she would. "You can't have him!" she burst out. "For a start he isn't ready yet…"

Max Satchwell interrupted her. "Not ready?" He looked swiftly at Lou. "But you told me on the telephone that this horse was looking for a new home."

Lou flushed. "I'm sorry … it seems I spoke too soon."

Carl cut in smoothly. "A slight misunderstanding. However, if your daughter wants the horse, a deposit will secure him for her, Mr Satchwell."

Amy stared at him in outrage. How *dare* he say that a deposit would secure Spartan! She swung round to Lou only to find that Lou was looking just as angry.

"A deposit will not secure him!" Lou said in a controlled voice. "Spartan will only go when we are sure we have found him the right home!" She turned to Mr Satchwell and to Amy's astonishment said, "I am sorry, truly I am, if I didn't explain things fully on the telephone. But we have a policy of selecting new homes for our horses very, very carefully. People cannot just come and choose a horse, particularly a horse like Spartan who has been so badly traumatized. He needs a quiet home with an experienced owner."

Max Satchwell looked outraged. "You mean, you're not going to let my daughter have this horse?"

Lou shook her head. "No, I'm afraid not." She smiled

quickly at Amy and then turned to Melanie, her eyes sympathetic. "Please try and understand, Melanie. I don't mean to be unfair, it's just that I don't think Spartan will be the right horse for you. We do have other horses you might be interested in though. There's..."

"You've already wasted enough of my time, Miss Fleming," Max Satchwell interrupted. "We'll be leaving right away!"

"Hold on, Daddy!" Melanie exclaimed suddenly. "I want to have a look at the other horses."

The Satchwells and Amy looked at her in amazement. Amy had been sure that she would stalk off when she was told that she couldn't have Spartan, but it seemed she had judged the girl wrongly.

Melanie walked over to her father. "They're right, Daddy," she said calmly. "I probably don't want a horse that I have to be really careful around the whole time. There might be another that isn't so nervous."

"Several, actually," Lou said, looking as if she couldn't believe her ears. "Aren't there, Amy?"

Amy nodded. "Do you want to come with me and have a look around?" she offered to Melanie. "You might like Copper – he's not at all nervous and he needs a good home with lots going on."

"Can I see him?" Melanie asked eagerly.

"Sure," Amy replied. "Come on." She set off with Melanie up the yard.

* * *

An hour later, Melanie had completely fallen in love with Copper. As Amy watched the younger girl ride him round the schooling ring, she smiled. Copper was a young horse that had been at Heartland for three months. He needed a fun, lively home and Amy felt sure that Melanie would look after him well.

"What do you think?" Ty said to her in a low voice.

"They're perfect for each other," Amy told him.

"I think so, too," Ty agreed, smiling at her.

After Melanie had dismounted and helped Amy untack Copper, the Satchwells booked a time the following week for Ty to come and check out the livery yard where Melanie kept her horse.

"Bye, Copper," Melanie said, kissing the chestnut on the nose. "See you soon."

Amy watched the Satchwells leave and then headed up to Spartan's stall. She stroked his bay head. She was really pleased for Copper, but she still wasn't any closer to finding the right home for Spartan.

For the rest of the day, Lou seemed cool around Carl. She could not seem to forgive him for his interference with the Satchwells. However, by the time it came for him to go back to Manhattan, Amy noticed that she had begun to relent.

"I'll miss you," Lou said, as Carl put his bag in his car.

Carl put his arm around her shoulders. "Promise me you'll really think about Chicago this week?"

"Yes," Lou said, looking up at him. "I will."

They kissed and then Carl got into the car. "See you on Friday," he said as he started the engine. "Don't wear yourself out with all those dance preparations."

Amy watched Lou stand and wave until Carl's sports car disappeared down the drive.

She couldn't help feeling disappointed. After the way Lou had been so supportive that afternoon and positively angry with Carl over Copper, she had begun to feel a real hope that Lou would turn down her boyfriend's offer and stay on at Heartland for good. Looking at Lou's face now, though, she didn't feel so sure.

Chapter Ten

The next day, Amy took Spartan out for another trail ride, taking care to stick to the paths where he would feel confident. Enjoying the sand and grass beneath his feet, he pulled at his reins and pranced excitedly. The track ahead was long and grassy so Amy leant forward and let him canter. Spartan's long strides seemed to eat up the ground. Ahead of them a fallen tree lay half across the path. Amy tightened her hold on the reins. "Easy now, boy," she said, intending to slow him down to a trot and pass around the tree trunk. Spartan tossed his head.

Amy felt excitement surge through her. He wanted to jump it. She knew she should take things slowly with him but the tree trunk looked so tempting. Although no one was there, she glanced around almost guiltily and then shortened her reins, turning him towards the low end of the tree trunk.

Spartan broke into a canter. Amy dug her knees into the saddle. They were three strides away, two, one, and then with a surge of power Spartan leapt into the air, clearing the log by nearly a metre.

"Wow!" Amy gasped, patting his neck. Spartan snorted and putting his head down bucked with sheer delight. Amy laughed and pulled his head up to stop him. He had felt amazing!

She patted him for a moment, knowing she should go on. Instead, she trotted him back round the tree trunk. This time when she turned Spartan she headed him for the highest part. As he plunged eagerly forward her heart leapt into her throat. What was she doing? But then she felt his smooth, powerful canter and her doubts disappeared. She sat down deep in the saddle. The tree trunk loomed in front of them and suddenly they were over.

"Good boy!" Amy cried ecstatically. She patted his neck over and over again, feeling excitement buzz through her. Spartan looked like he was a natural jumper.

Amy didn't stay on the trail for long. She was keen to tell Ty about Spartan's jumping.

"He was so good!" she told Ty, having found him the moment she got back. "He just flew over it both times!"

"You should try him in the training ring tomorrow," Ty said.

"That's a great idea!" Amy said, feeling exhilarated by the thought.

* * *

The next day, after schooling Spartan on the flat Amy hitched him to a post and put up a small jump. As she remounted she felt a flicker of nervousness. Maybe the day before had just been a fluke. Spartan cleared the jump easily, though, and Amy put it up higher just as Ty arrived to watch.

"Wow!" he said, as Spartan cleared the jump by half a metre.

"He feels like he wants to go higher and higher," said Amy, her eyes shining. "He's brilliant!"

From then on, every time that Amy rode Spartan she put up a jump. On Friday afternoon, she got Ty to help her set out a whole course of fences. "Here goes!" she called to him after she had worked Spartan in for a while.

Spartan threw his head up as she turned him into the first jump but he soon settled into a perfect rhythm. He cleared jump after jump, and was evidently enjoying himself.

As they were approaching the last one, Amy suddenly realized that she had only ever felt such sheer ability in one other horse, and that was Pegasus. Excitement flooded through her. Spartan was smaller than Pegasus, but was there any reason why he shouldn't one day be as good a jumper?

As they cleared the last jump, Ty clapped. "That was incredible!" he said.

"I know!" Amy replied, her cheeks glowing. She looked round at the jumps. "I'd love to take him in a show – do a proper long course of jumps. I bet he'd be fantastic!"

"Well, I guess he's not ready to compete yet, but there is a show on at The Meadows showground on Sunday," Ty said. "You could always take him along. Get him used to the atmosphere."

Amy stared at him. "Yes!" she said. "And they have a schooling ring there. You can pay to go round a course of jumps. It would be a brilliant experience for him!"

"Good idea," Ty said.

Amy's face suddenly fell. "I bet Grandpa won't drive me — it will be the day after the dance and he'll be busy helping Lou with the clearing up."

"I'll drive you if you want," Ty offered.

"Really?" Amy said. "But it's your day off."

Ty grinned. "I guess I can cope — after all, it's for a good cause. You never know — if he jumps really well then we might just find someone who would give him a good home when he's ready."

Amy nodded, her thoughts reeling. She was going to take Spartan to a show! It seemed incredible that it was only a matter of days since he wouldn't even let her anywhere near him.

After Amy had put Spartan away in his box she went to the tack-room to clean his tack. She went back to check on him when she had finished. He was lying down in his stall, muzzle resting on the clean straw, legs curled underneath him like a dog. Amy smiled and quietly opened the door. Spartan looked at her but didn't get up.

"Having a rest, are you?" she murmured, kneeling down beside him in the straw and stroking his neck. Spartan snorted and rested his muzzle on her lap. Her fingers played in his mane and he relaxed, his eyes half closing, his lips splaying slightly as he let her legs take the weight of his head.

Amy closed her eyes for a moment, letting her dreams play out in her head. She imagined Spartan, clearing fence after fence at some big show, his scars not mattering, everyone cheering for him as he won class after class. He would be confident, happy. She let the most secret of her dreams come to the surface. Him living at Heartland, staying with her. Although she knew that the horses who came to Heartland had to be re-homed, Spartan was different. In her imagination, they galloped around an arena, a blue ribbon flying from Spartan's bridle. One day, they might even become as good a partnership as Daddy and Pegasus had once been.

She opened her eyes. "It could be," she whispered. "You and me, Spartan. I think we were meant to be together. I understand you better than anyone else ever could."

Spartan blew softly out through his nose.

"You'll be happy with me," Amy said, kissing his head. "I'll *make* you happy." Feeling a great rush of affection, she put her arms round his neck and hugged him. As she did so she looked him in the eyes. His dark brown eyes were full of trust, but something was missing – it was *love*.

Amy's arms slackened their grip. She knew people were

wrong, when they said that horses couldn't feel love. When she looked into Pegasus's or Sundance's eyes she could see love reflected there, welling deep and strong from the centre of their being. Spartan's eyes just held a sadness that hadn't gone away despite all her love for him.

He nuzzled her, but at that moment she realized that her dreams would always be just that – *dreams*. She could not bring the light back into his eyes. A lump formed in Amy's throat as she faced the bitter truth. Spartan was only hers for a little while – hers on loan, not hers to keep.

She stood up and walked slowly out of his stall.

"Amy! Amy!"

Amy looked up. There, jogging up the driveway with her black curls bouncing, was Soraya!

"Soraya!" Amy gasped. She had been so busy thinking about Spartan that she had forgotten Soraya was due back that day. Throwing off her worries, she raced down the yard to meet her friend. "You're home!"

"I'd noticed," Soraya grinned, and they hugged. As they separated, Soraya looked round. "Gee, it's good to be back." Her eyes sparkled. "Not that I didn't enjoy camp, of course."

Amy grinned. "It sounds like you enjoyed it rather too much! So who's this Chris you kept going on about in your letters?"

"Chris?" Soraya said. "Amy, you're way out of date! For the last two weeks I've been going out with Kyle." She shook her head. "I can see you and me have got some serious catching up to do!"

One hour and a bag of chocolate and pecan biscuits later, Amy and Soraya had just about caught up with each other's news. Soraya had started going out with a boy called Kyle after a barbecue one night at riding camp, but as they lived hours away from each other they had decided not to continue dating once they returned home.

"He was nice, though," Soraya said slightly wistfully as she showed Amy his photo. "And he is going to write."

Amy hugged her. "You'll meet someone round here." She saw Soraya's disbelieving face. "I know you will!"

"All the halfway decent boys round here are either attached or madly in love with someone else," Soraya said. She shook her head at Amy. "Talking of which – what's going on with you and Matt?"

Amy shook her head. "Oh, the same as usual. We're just good friends."

"He'll start going out with someone else soon," Soraya warned.

"Maybe you," Amy teased her.

"As if that's likely!" Soraya said. "I was thinking more of Ashley Grant – she's had her eye on Matt for ages."

"Well, she's coming to the barn dance tomorrow," Amy said, pulling a face. "I bet she'll wear something amazing to catch his eye."

"It'll probably have cost something amazing too," Soraya said, shifting into a more comfortable position on Amy's bed. "So, how are all the preparations for the dance going? Is there much left to do?"

"Loads," Amy said. "We had a whole bunch of stuff delivered at lunchtime that needs sorting out, and there's about a million napkins to be folded. Tomorrow is going to be just crazy!"

"I'll help with it all," Soraya offered. "I think it's a really cool idea — having the dance, I mean."

"Yeah, I do now," Amy admitted. "I wasn't that keen at first but lots of people have been buying tickets. I guess Lou was right about it being a good way to raise money and bring Mom's friends up here."

Soraya looked at her shrewdly. They had been friends for a long time and she knew Amy and Lou's stormy relationship well. "How have you guys been getting on?"

Amy thought for a moment. "Better," she said. "We've been arguing on and off but over the last few days things have improved."

"You said in your last letter that Lou was thinking of moving to Chicago," Soraya said. "And by the way, may I remind you that we said we'd write at least three times a week. Not the one letter every ten days or so that I actually got."

"I know — I'm sorry! It's just been crazy around here," Amy said. She shook her head. "Lou's still thinking about going to Chicago. I don't want her to, but she's just so into Carl that I think she might."

"And you still don't like him?"

Amy sighed. "I feel bad about that because I know he makes Lou happy ... there's just something about him..." Amy heard a car outside and looked out of the window. "Speaking of Carl, here he is."

"Come on, I want to meet him," Soraya said, jumping up and heading for the door.

Amy followed her. "You don't. You really don't."

They went downstairs just as Carl came in. "I saw your post had arrived," he said, handing a pile of letters to Jack Bartlett. "So I thought I'd bring it up with me."

"Thanks, Carl," Grandpa said. "How was your journey?"

"Good, thanks," Carl replied. He nodded at Amy and Soraya. "Hi there, kids."

"Hi," Soraya said politely, and then when Carl looked away she mimed being sick.

Amy nodded. *Kids!* How old did Carl think they were?

Soraya smiled at her. "I'd better get back home. I promised Mom I wouldn't stay long. But I'll come round in the morning and help."

"OK," Amy said, walking to the door with her. "See you tomorrow. It's great to have you back!"

She watched Soraya disappear down the driveway and then went into the kitchen. Carl had his arm round Lou.

"We've got so much to do!" Lou was saying to him. "I'm

glad you're here."

"Don't worry. With you in charge it's bound to be a perfect success," Carl said smoothly. "So, how many people are coming?"

"Eighty-two at the last count," Lou said.

Carl looked casually at the post. "And I guess a few more replies might have come today."

Lou picked up the pile to check. "Yes, it looks like it." Amy was about to go back upstairs when she heard Lou's voice change. "Hey, what's this?" Lou held up an envelope and frowned.

"Anything interesting?" Carl said, looking over her shoulder.

"It's from Epstein and Webb," Lou said, holding in her hands a smart cream envelope with an embossed crest. "What are they writing to me for?"

"Well, open it and see," said Carl.

Amy glanced at him. The slightest of smiles was playing at the corners of his lips.

Lou tore open the envelope and took out a letter. She read down it, her eyes widening. Suddenly she gasped. "They've offered me a job!" she cried, looking up. "An amazing one. And it's in Chicago." Lou flung her arms around Carl's neck. "It's actually in Chicago!"

"What? That's incredible!" Carl exclaimed. He hugged her. "It's fate, Lou. We were obviously meant to be together in Chicago. Just think — we can get a flat together, start a new life!"

"Oh, Carl!" Lou cried.

"Congratulations, Lou," Grandpa said quietly.

Amy saw the sadness in his eyes.

Lou seemed to see it too. She froze, the excitement fading quickly from her face. "Well, of course I haven't decided if I'll take it yet," she said hastily, stuffing the letter in her pocket and looking rather awkwardly from Grandpa to Amy.

"*If* you'll take it?" Carl stared at her incredulously. "Lou, this is the opportunity of a lifetime! You can't tell me you're thinking of turning it down?"

"It's a big move," Lou said defensively.

"Lou!" Carl said in exasperation.

"Please, Carl," Lou said. "I need to think about it."

Carl stared at her for a moment, his face tightening. Suddenly he picked up his bag. "I'm going to get changed," he said abruptly, striding out of the kitchen.

Lou sat down at the table. "Oh, Grandpa," she sighed. As she looked up, Amy saw the confusion in her eyes. "What am I going to do?"

"What do you want to do?" Grandpa said, sitting down opposite her

"That's just it ... I don't know."

"Don't take it, Lou. Stay here with us," Amy said softly, sitting down next to her.

"I *am* beginning to love it here. But I love Carl too," Lou said. She shook her head. "And anyway, you don't need me."

"We do!" Amy burst out.

"No, Amy. You don't," Lou said. "I make mistakes like with the feed merchants and trying to find homes for horses before they're ready. And you don't listen to my ideas and that's hard. I'm used to being respected, I'm used to having my ideas really count."

"I *will* listen and we *do* need you," Amy said desperately.

Lou looked round distractedly. "Please, Grandpa," she groaned. "Tell me what to do."

"I can't do that, honey," Jack Bartlett said, shaking his head. "You need to decide for yourself."

Lou sighed. "I know. But how?"

Grandpa came over and kissed her head. "Just follow your heart, Lou," he said softly. "Follow your heart."

Chapter Eleven

"If I see one more red napkin I am going to go crazy!" Soraya declared as she folded a set of cutlery into the last napkin and put it down on the table with a bang. "What else do we need to do?"

Amy looked up from unpacking a crate of glasses. "There's one more table to be put up," she said, "and then the cloths need to go on them all."

As she spoke, Matt came through the doorway carrying the last one. "Where do you want this?" he asked.

"Over there," Amy said, pointing to a gap. "Thanks, Matt."

"So, what's happening about the food?" Matt asked as he set out the table.

"Well, Grandpa collected the meat for the barbecue yesterday and he and Lou are making loads of salads and desserts," Amy said. She had been put in charge of organizing the barn while Carl went off to collect the drinks for the evening. She thought about the show the next day. She wasn't going to get a chance to groom Spartan. Despite the late night ahead, she'd just have to get up early in the morning and get him ready then.

"What next?" Matt said, coming over.

"If you unpack the plates," Amy said, pointing to the boxes of hired crockery, "I'll go and see if Carl has arrived with the drinks."

She went through to the kitchen. "Is Carl back?"

"Just," Lou said, looking up from slicing a tomato. "He's still outside."

Amy went out. Carl was leaning against the pick-up with his back to her. Amy realized that he was speaking on his mobile phone. She walked over quietly, intending to start unloading – she didn't want to disturb him.

She heard Carl laugh. "Of course she doesn't know," he said. "She doesn't suspect a thing." Amy was trying not to listen but his next words pulled her up short. "No, no. You've got her all wrong," he said. "Lou's not naïve; she just trusts me." Amy froze at the mention of her sister's name. Carl shook his head. "The trouble with Lou is that she just doesn't realize what will make her happy. All I've done is nudge her in the right direction – given fate a helping hand, if you like."

Amy started to back slowly away. Her mind was reeling. It sounded like this job offer in Chicago was a set-up!

Carl knew about it and was pretending he didn't. Amy suddenly remembered the way he had urged Lou to look through the post the day before. She had to tell Lou what she knew!

Just then her foot caught on a stone and she tripped. Carl looked round. "Amy!" he said.

"Er ... hi," Amy said. "I was just coming to help carry the drinks inside."

Carl visibly relaxed. "Oh, right." He spoke into his phone. "I'll speak to you later, Brett. Bye."

All the time Amy was helping Carl unload the drinks, she was desperate to go and find Lou to tell her what she suspected. However, when they had finished, she lost her chance to speak to her sister alone because Carl followed her into the kitchen.

Unfortunately, Lou was busy all day and Amy couldn't find a moment to talk to her without someone interrupting. In the end she tried to push what she had heard to the back of her mind, deciding to tell Lou about it the next day when things were quieter and her sister was less stressed.

By six o'clock, the barn was almost ready. The decorations were finished, the barbecue was lit, Grandpa had made his special punch and the raffle tickets were stacked up, ready to be sold.

"Time to get changed!" Lou called, running through the kitchen. "It won't be long before people start arriving!"

Matt had gone home, but Soraya had brought her clothes round so that she could get changed with Amy.

"What do you think Ashley will be wearing?" she asked as she sat at Amy's mirror and teased out her dark curls.

"Something revealing," Amy said. She looked over Soraya's shoulder and twisted her hair up. "What do you reckon – up or down?"

"Up!" Soraya said. She got to her feet and helped Amy secure her thick light-brown hair. "There!" she said, pulling down a few strands so that they framed Amy's face.

"Yeah, I like it," Amy said, pleased. She took out a pair of midnight-blue cropped trousers from her wardrobe and pulled them on. Her mom had them bought them for her a year ago. She had hardly had a chance to wear them and luckily they still fitted, hugging her slim figure from her hips to her mid-calves.

"Wow! Matt won't be able to keep his hands off you in those!" Soraya giggled as Amy looked at herself in the mirror. She pulled on a pair of black jeans and a strappy top made out of a silvery material. "How do I look?" she said, posing.

"Great!" Amy said. "Come on! Let's go!"

They hurried down the stairs and into the kitchen. Grandpa, Carl and Ty were already there.

"You both look wonderful!" Grandpa said.

"Thank you," Soraya said.

Amy looked at Ty. He looked darkly handsome, his checked shirt emphasizing his lithe, muscular shoulders.

"Wow!" he said, looking Amy up and down. "You look stunning!"

Amy raised her eyebrows teasingly. "You mean I don't usually?"

"It's certainly a change from your yard jeans," Ty commented. He grinned at her. "You really do look nice."

"Thanks." She smiled. "So do you." Their eyes met. Then Amy glanced away, feeling suddenly flustered.

Lou came into the kitchen from the barn. "I hope everyone turns up," she fretted.

Jack Bartlett opened the refrigerator and pulled out a jug of punch. "A toast!" he declared, getting out a tray of glasses. He filled the glasses and passed them round. "To the success of the dance!"

Amy looked at her sister. "To Lou!" she said impulsively.

"To Lou!" everyone echoed, clinking their glasses.

Lou smiled round happily. "Thank you," she said.

"Right," Jack Bartlett said. "We can't just stand around. There's nibbles to be put out, drinks to be poured and parking to be organized."

Ty finished his glass and went outside to deal with the parking. Amy set about opening packets of crisps while Soraya went with Jack Bartlett to the barn to help with the drinks.

Lou was just about to follow them when Carl caught her arm. "Here," he said, picking up their glasses and refilling them with punch. "Let's have another toast."

Amy glanced up.

"What to?" Lou asked.

Carl raised his glass. "To Chicago!"

Amy saw Lou falter, her glass stopping halfway to her mouth. "I still haven't decided whether I'm going yet, Carl."

Words leapt to Amy's lips but she bit them back.

"Lou!" Carl exclaimed. "This is the perfect job, the perfect opportunity for us to be together. How can you still be undecided?"

"It's a hard decision to make," Lou said. "Surely you can see that? I need more time to think about it."

"You don't have the time!" Carl said, sounding irritated. "They want a decision by Tuesday."

"I know! I know!" Lou suddenly stopped. Amy saw her frown. "How do you know they want a decision by Tuesday?" she said to Carl. "I didn't tell you."

For an instant, Carl looked horror-struck but his expression quickly smoothed. "Of course you did," he said, putting a hand on her arm. "You must've forgotten."

"I didn't." Lou exclaimed. "I didn't want to tell you in case you started to pressurize me again. How did you know?" She suddenly took a step back, her eyes widening, her face going pale. "*You arranged it, didn't you?*" she whispered. "You *knew* about this job all along."

Carl looked for a moment as if he was going to deny it but then he stepped forward. "Well, so what if I did?" he said. "Yes, OK, I arranged it, Lou. I want you to come with me – people *expect* you to come with me."

"You want me to come because of what our friends would think if I didn't!" Lou stared at him in horror.

"No ... I..." Carl hastily changed tack. "Lou, I only tried to get you a good job," he said, grabbing her hand. "Is that such a huge crime?"

"You tried to manipulate me! You deceived me!" Lou cried, snatching her hand away.

"Lou, listen..."

"No!" Lou shouted. "I trusted you, Carl! How could you do this to me?"

Just then the back door opened and Scott and Matt walked in. Their greetings died on their lips as they took in the situation.

"Lou..." Carl moved forward.

Lou pushed him away. "Don't touch me!" she hissed. "Get out of my sight! I'm not coming to Chicago with you. I never, *ever* want to see you again!"

"But..."

"Just go, Carl!" Lou shouted. "Go!" With that she burst into tears and ran out of the room.

Amy jumped to her feet but before she could say anything Scott stepped forward. "You heard Lou," he said icily to Carl. "I think you'd better leave."

For a moment it looked as if Carl was about to hit him but then he took a step back. "I'll get my things!" he snapped and then turning on his heel he stalked upstairs.

Scott looked out of the window. "Amy! Quick! The guests are arriving."

Amy looked at him in horror. "What about Lou...?"

"You go," Scott said. "Matt and I will sort things out down here."

As Amy ran up the stairs, Carl came pushing past her, shoving things into his bag as he went.

"Bye to you too," Amy muttered.

She hurried to Lou's bedroom. Her sister was lying face-down on the bed.

"Oh, Amy!" she sobbed, looking up. "What am I going to do?" She buried her head in her hands.

"You have to do what you think is right for you," Amy faltered. "Do you really want Carl to go to Chicago without you?"

Lou turned towards her sister. "All I know is that after all that's happened these past few months ... I definitely don't need anyone around who I can't trust."

Amy knelt on the floor beside the bed and stroked Lou's hair. "Then I guess you're right," she said. "You are better off without him."

"How could he do that to me?" Lou cried. "I thought he respected me. I thought he *loved* me."

Amy wrapped her arms round her. "Oh, Lou, Lou, we love you!" she said desperately. "Whatever you decide, Grandpa and I will always be here for you. No matter whether you stay here or go back to New York, this will always be your home."

Lou started to sob even harder.

"And look, don't worry about the dance," Amy gabbled. "We'll manage. Scott's sorting out the guests. Everything is under control."

Lou sat up, tears running down her cheeks. "People are arriving already?"

Amy nodded. "But don't worry," she said quickly. "We can cope. You stay up here for as long as you want."

Lou brushed her tears away, "I organized it. I should be there."

"Lou…"

"I'll be OK." With a sniff, Lou stood up and smoothed down her dress.

Amy felt her heart fill with admiration. *Lou is so strong*, she thought. She knew if their positions had been reversed she would have stayed in her room all night, crying her eyes out. Now Lou was already looking into the mirror and fixing her make-up.

When she finally straightened up, the only hint of her inner turmoil was the tear-washed brightness of her eyes. "Come on," she said, taking a deep breath and reaching for Amy's hand. "Our friends will be waiting."

Amy hurried about filling up glasses and saying hi. She tried to keep an eye on Lou to make sure she was OK. There was no need to worry, though. With a bright smile on her face she greeted people, fetched them drinks and steered them towards the table where Ty was selling raffle tickets.

The Grant family arrived, Ashley looking stunning in a short green dress that had virtually no back.

Very suitable for a barn dance, Amy thought sarcastically.

"Hello, Amy," Ashley said coolly.

"Hi," Amy replied, her voice curt.

Ashley looked round, her perfect eyebrows arching in surprise. "You've really got quite a few people here, haven't you?"

"That *was* the idea," Amy retorted, but Ashley wasn't listening. She had spotted Matt.

"Matt!" she called.

He looked round and came over. "Hi, Ashley," he said pleasantly.

"Hi," said Ashley, putting her arm through his. "Do you know where the drinks are?"

"Sure," Matt said in surprise. "Come on, I'll show you."

Shaking her head in amusement, Amy hurried away. Even Ashley's presence couldn't spoil the evening.

The barn filled up quickly. The noise level rose, glasses clinked, and as the band started up people began moving on to the dance floor. Amy realized how right Lou had been all along. This was a brilliant way to raise money! Everyone seemed to be having a wonderful time and it was great to see all Mom's friends. Amy thought about how proud Mom would have been of her eldest daughter.

She looked round for Lou and spotted her standing with Grandpa and Scott by the entrance to the barn. The strain on her face from earlier had vanished completely. Scott said something and Lou laughed up at him, her eyes sparkling.

She looked genuinely happy and delighted as she watched all the guests having a good time.

Amy hurried over. "Lou! This is such a success — everyone's really enjoying themselves."

"They certainly are," Scott agreed. "Congratulations, Lou!"

"Thanks," Lou smiled. "And thanks for all your help."

"I'm sorry I doubted you," Amy said impulsively.

Lou looked slightly taken aback by her apology. "Thanks, Amy."

"And..." Amy struggled, finding the words difficult to say, "and ... I think some of your other ideas for Heartland might work too. You know, the brochure and things like that."

"Really?" Lou stared. "You'd really give them a chance?"

Amy nodded. "I've realized you know what you're doing when it comes to money." She looked at her sister, the words tumbling impulsively out of her. "Look, I was stupid not to listen to you before. Please say you'll stay, Lou. I promise I'll take your ideas on board from now on. Don't go back to the city. Your home is here. We *need* you here."

Lou looked astonished and pleased. "Do you mean that?"

"Of course I do!" Amy cried.

Lou looked at Grandpa, Scott and Amy. "OK," she said, a smile suddenly spreading across her face. "I'll stay!"

Chapter Twelve

The last guests finally left the party in the early hours of the morning, and Amy finally collapsed in bed. She glanced at her alarm clock as she turned off her light. Two o'clock! In only four hours she had to be up again to get Spartan groomed and ready for the show. "Oh, great," she groaned, turning over and falling asleep.

At six o'clock, Amy dragged herself out of bed and staggered on to the yard. First there were the other horses to be fed and then Spartan to attend to. However, by drinking several cups of coffee she gradually managed to wake herself up and by the time Ty arrived at eight-thirty she was beginning to feel more cheerful. "You're going to be so good today," she told Spartan as she bandaged his tail to protect it in the trailer. "We'll show everyone just how special you are."

Spartan looked round at her and snorted, almost as though he understood.

When they arrived at the show Ty parked the trailer near the edge of the show-ground, well away from the main hubbub of the show rings and spectator stands. Spartan backed down the ramp and looked about excitedly, his ears pricked, his nostrils dilated.

"It's OK," Amy told him. "It's just a showground. Do you remember, boy?"

Ty bent down to remove Spartan's protective leg wraps. "I'd take him for a walk round," he said, throwing them in a pile and then removing the tail bandage. "It will help him settle."

Amy nodded. She'd been thinking the same thing. "Come on, then," she said, clicking her tongue. "Let's go."

Spartan pranced beside her, his neck arched. Amy guessed he must remember going to shows with his previous owner. "And soon you might be going to shows again," she told him. "Not to go in boring conformation classes on the flat, though – in jumping classes so that everyone can see how good you are."

Just then, a rider cantered straight across their path only a couple of metres in front of them. Spartan shied back in surprise. "Steady, boy!" Amy exclaimed.

She swung round.

It was Ashley Grant, sitting astride a bay pony, looking

smug, her clothes perfect and her pony gleaming. Even though she'd had a late night, Ashley looked as fresh as a daisy. "He's still nervous, then!" she said.

"Any horse would be nervous if you did that to it!" Amy exclaimed.

"Temper, temper," Ashley mocked.

Amy shook her head in disgust and walked Spartan on. She ran her hand up and down his neck to keep him calm.

However, there was no escaping Ashley. She rode alongside Spartan. "So, what have you brought *him* here for?" she said. "I heard he was vicious."

"Well, he's not," Amy said, through gritted teeth. "He's healed."

Ashley laughed as she looked at Spartan's sides. "His scars certainly aren't!"

"So?" Amy demanded.

"So, you're not exactly going to get far with him in the show ring, are you?" Ashley said.

"I'm not planning to take him in conformation," Amy retorted. "And you know that in jumping classes scars don't matter."

"Like a judge is *really* going to pick a horse with scars like that," Ashley said. She shook her head. "You're wasting your time and your money, Amy — and from what *I've* heard, Heartland hasn't got too much cash to spare just at the moment." With a mocking smile she cantered off.

"Just you wait till you see him jump, Ashley," Amy

muttered. She suddenly felt a strong desire to enter Spartan in a class just so that she could wipe the smile off Ashley's perfect face. But entries had closed a week ago. "Next time," she promised Spartan as she watched Ashley enter the collecting ring on the bay pony.

Amy took Spartan back to the trailer. "I think I'll get on," she said to Ty. "He seems fine."

They tacked Spartan up. Amy pulled off the tracksuit bottoms that she had been wearing to keep her beige show breeches clean, and pulled on her long boots and navy jacket. It felt good to be in show clothes again.

"Just take it steadily," Ty said, holding the opposite stirrup as she mounted. "You don't want to overdo it."

Amy nodded. As she patted Spartan she felt sure that he would be fine – he felt excited but not wild. She entered the schooling area where the other horses and riders were warming up. There were trainers shouting instructions, ponies shooting past. Amy took a breath. If Spartan could cope with this then he could cope with anything!

At first he was a little highly strung, but after ten minutes or so, once he was settled, he started to listen to her aids. Amy tried him over a jump. He didn't even hesitate. After they had warmed up over several small fences, Amy decided it was time to take him over a course in the schooling ring.

Ty saw her heading for the entrance and walked round to meet her. "He looks good. You think he's ready?"

Amy nodded, excitement gathering in the pit of her stomach. This was the moment she had been waiting for.

At the gate to the training ring Ty paid the official the schooling fee. "Are the jumps OK at this height?" the official asked. Ty turned to Amy.

Amy looked around the elaborate course. The jumps were just over a metre, higher than she would have ideally liked, but when she sat on Spartan she felt as if she could jump anything! "They're fine," she said.

"Good luck!" Ty called as she rode into the ring.

Shortening her reins, Amy patted Spartan's neck. "This is it, boy," she said, her excitement growing as she noticed a few spectators watching casually at the fence. "Let's show everyone what you can do."

Spartan's ears flickered. She closed her legs on his sides and he moved forward into a smooth canter. Amy circled once and then turned into the first jump – an imposing post and rails. Spartan's stride pattern was even and perfect. He cleared the fence easily, his ears pricked forward as he headed to the second fence in the outside line.

Amy stayed with his steady rhythm as they cleared fence after fence. She could hardly believe what a great understanding they had. She cantered him towards the final jump – a parallel spread – right next to the ring.

"Gerry?" she heard a girl's voice gasp from the ringside. Amy felt Spartan falter. They were only three strides away from the fence and they had too much momentum to pull away. Amy closed her legs around his sides and pushed him on. "Come on, boy," she whispered. Spartan responded. With an enormous surge of power he gathered himself and took off over the fence. It seemed like a minute had passed before they landed safely on the other side.

There was a smattering of applause from those watching.

"Good boy!" Amy cried, forgetting about the voice from the crowd in her sheer delight. Patting him constantly she trotted over to the gate. "Wasn't he great?" she cried to Ty.

"The best!" Ty called back.

"A very nice round," the official said to Amy. "You've got a horse there with a lot of potential, young lady. You're sure to come away with lots of ribbons."

Amy smiled as she slid off Spartan's back and flung her arms round his neck. "You were wonderful!" she said. Then, taking Spartan's reins, she led him away with Ty.

"Um ... excuse me," a voice said tentatively behind them.

Amy looked round. A girl of about her own age with wavy dark hair was standing there. She was dressed in show clothes and her cheeks looked slightly flushed. "Is that Gerry ... Geronimo?"

"Yes," Amy said in confusion, turning Spartan round. "At least he *was*. Who are you?"

Before the girl had a chance to reply, Spartan nickered and dragged Amy forward with a toss of his head.

"Oh, Gerry," the girl breathed in delight. "I thought I was never going to see you again."

Amy felt a spasm of jealousy as Spartan nuzzled the girl's hands. Who was she? "Um ... sorry, but I don't know who you are," she said rather shortly.

The girl looked up at her, her blue eyes suddenly flustered. "I'm Hannah Boswell. Larry Boswell's my grandfather. I've known Gerry since he was born. I recognized him as soon as you came into the ring."

Amy's eyes widened in astonishment. "You're Mr Boswell's granddaughter?"

Hannah nodded. "I live on the farm with him and Grandma. Are you Amy?" When Amy nodded Hannah smiled. "Grandpa told me about you. About your rescue centre and how you've been looking after Gerry."

"What are you doing here?" Amy said, still trying to get her head round meeting Larry Boswell's granddaughter.

"I'm here for the show," Hannah said. "I was supposed to be going in an equitation class."

Ty frowned. "I thought I'd seen you before," he said. "Have you got a dapple-grey pony?"

"That's right," Hannah said. "We don't travel this far all the time, only when there's a big class on like today's."

"You're really good," Ty said. "I saw you at Middlebrook." Amy felt a flash of jealousy as Hannah smiled at Ty.

"Thanks," the other girl said. "I'm just lucky I've got Sinbad." Her eyes glowed. "He'd make any rider look wonderful."

Amy's jealousy disappeared as she heard Hannah Boswell

praising her pony and she felt herself warming to her. "What did you mean, you were *supposed* to be going in for an equitation class?" she asked curiously.

"Sinbad's gone lame," Hannah said. "He must have knocked himself on the ride over. It's not really bad, but I'm not going to risk riding him. I'm just going to cancel my entry. It's typical, though, that it's happened when there's a big qualifying class." Although she smiled, Amy saw that her eyes looked sad. She looked round. "I must tell my grandma that you're here. I know she'll want to say hello. Is that OK?" she asked.

"Yeah, sure," Amy said.

"I'll be back in a minute," Hannah promised, setting off across the show ground.

"She seems nice," Amy said, turning to Ty. She didn't compete in equitation herself, preferring the hunter division where the emphasis was on the horse and not the rider. Still, she knew Hannah must be disappointed.

Ty nodded. "She's a really talented rider," he said. "Got a real gift. Whatever she might say that pony of hers doesn't look easy to ride."

Amy patted Spartan thoughtfully. She thought about what Hannah had said about her pony being lame.

Hannah came running back. "Grandma's coming!" she panted, her dark hair tousled. Spartan pulled towards her and nuzzled her.

"Um..." Amy took a deep breath, the idea spilling out of

her. "Hannah, would you like to ride Spartan — I mean *Gerry* — in the equitation class?"

She saw Ty turn and stare at her. Hannah's eyes widened. "Ride Gerry? But you don't even know if I can ride!" Hannah said.

"Well, Ty's seen you and he says you're good," Amy said. She glanced at Ty. "That's enough for me to go on."

"Well, I'd love to ride him!" Hannah said. She scanned Amy's face anxiously. "You really wouldn't mind?"

"No," Amy said slowly, watching as Spartan breathed on Hannah's hand. "No, I wouldn't mind."

Hannah smiled and then suddenly waved at someone over Amy's shoulder. "Grandma! I'm here!"

Mrs Boswell had short grey hair and was dressed in jeans. Her face lit up as she saw Spartan. "Gerry!" she said.

Spartan nickered softly. Mrs Boswell smiled and rubbed his head. "Well, hi, boy. It's sure good to see you looking so well." She turned to Amy and Ty, holding out her hand and smiling. "Hello there, I'm Shelley Boswell."

They shook hands and introduced themselves. Hannah quickly explained about riding Spartan in the equitation class. "I'd better get my hat and saddle," she said. "My class is next."

"I'll ride Spartan round," Amy said. "Get him warmed up for you." She mounted.

"And I'll grab a brush so we can go over him before you enter the ring," Ty said. Amy nodded and rode Spartan into the schooling area. He trotted round, his strides long and smooth, his ears flickering as he listened to her aids. She asked him to canter and rode him in two neat figures of eight. "Good boy," she whispered, stroking his neck.

Seeing that Hannah had returned with her saddle, she brought him back to a walk and rode over to where Hannah stood.

"Is it OK if I use my saddle?" Hannah asked.

Amy nodded and dismounted. Taking a deep breath, she ran up the stirrups, undid the girth and then slid her saddle from Spartan's back.

"Are you still sure this is OK?" Hannah asked, looking at her.

Amy swallowed. "I'm sure."

She held Spartan's reins as Hannah lifted her own saddle on to Spartan's back. Spartan nuzzled her hands while Hannah did up the girth. Amy quickly kissed his nose.

"I really appreciate it," Hannah said, standing back. "It's my last chance to qualify for the state finals."

Feeling her heart twist, Amy held out Spartan's reins to Hannah. Their eyes met.

"Good luck," Amy whispered, still holding on.

"Thank you," Hannah said softly.

Slowly, Amy let go.

After Hannah had ridden round for a bit and had taken Spartan over a few jumps, she came over to Ty and Amy. Ty gave Spartan a quick brush over. "You look good on him," he said.

Amy nodded. She had been watching carefully as Hannah rode round and had quickly seen that Ty was right. Hannah was a very talented rider – her hands were light and her seat was perfectly balanced. Spartan looked relaxed and happy.

"I always loved riding him when he was at Grandpa's," Hannah said. She smiled. "He feels strange after Sinbad, though."

"How many hands is Sinbad?" Amy asked.

"Fourteen-two and getting a bit too small for me now. Grandpa's said he'll buy me a new horse, but I just can't find one I really like." She smiled. "I'll keep Sinbad as well, of course. I'll never sell him."

Shelley Boswell came over. "Hannah! You need to report to the announcer so they know you're here."

Hannah grinned nervously. "Well, here goes. Wish me luck!"

"Oh, Hannah?" Amy said. Hannah looked back. "If he seems to hesitate before a fence, give him a tiny nudge and he'll be fine. He just needs a little reassurance sometimes."

Hannah nodded. "Thanks," she said.

Ty and Amy went to watch at the ringside. "Look, it's Ashley!" Amy said, nudging Ty as Ashley trotted into the ring. She was now on a different horse – a beautiful grey with a tail that floated out behind it like a waterfall. Ashley asked the pony to canter and headed smoothly towards the first jump.

Amy watched carefully. When she competed with Sundance against Ashley it was usually in the pony hunter classes. Equitation was different. It was the rider's style and ability that mattered, and Amy had to admit it – Ashley was good. She had perfect posture and her smile never left her face. "She doesn't seem to do anything wrong!" she said aloud.

"I don't know," Ty said critically. "She's a bit stiff in the shoulders."

At the next jump Ashley's horse took off too late.

"She'll lose points there," Ty commented.

"Not many," Amy said.

"You know, she hasn't got that real empathy with the horse, though," Ty said. "I mean, she's riding technically well but there's no bond there. The judges look for that as well as technical skill."

Ashley finished the course with a circle and rode out.

"Is it Hannah next?" Amy asked.

There was one more competitor first – a boy on a chestnut pony.

Shelley Boswell came to join them. "It was really kind of you to let Hannah ride Gerry," she said to Amy.

"That's OK," Amy said.

"Larry told me what happened on his visit to you. You must think he's not very devoted to his horses," Shelley Boswell said.

Amy wasn't sure what to say. "Well ... er..."

"It's all right, honey," Shelley Boswell said, smiling. "I can imagine what he must have been like. Larry's not a cruel man, despite what you might think. All his life he's had to work hard. He built the business up from scratch and he's always had the rule that each of the horses has to pay its way. That's what's made him successful. I think it broke his heart to let Gerry go, and he sure does miss him a lot. We all do."

"Hannah's up!" Ty said as the chestnut pony left the ring and Hannah trotted in.

Spartan's ears were pricked. He threw his head up for a moment as he saw the fences, but then listened to Hannah's aids and lowered his head. They moved smoothly into a canter and then turned towards the first jump.

Amy held her breath as Spartan sailed over it easily with loads to spare.

"He jumps big, doesn't he?" Shelley Boswell said.

Amy nodded. She was full of admiration for Hannah's riding. It wasn't easy to stay in the perfect position on a horse that jumped as high as Spartan but Hannah managed it. Her back was straight, her head up and her heels down. "Hannah looks really good on him," she said.

Shelley Boswell nodded. "Hannah loves jumping – always has. She's going to look for a horse to compete in the jumper division next."

Amy nodded, concentrating on the ring. Hannah and Spartan were halfway round the course now. As they cantered round the far side of the ring they made a perfect picture. There appeared to be a bond between them, a special quality that shone out – they seemed to understand each other. Amy suddenly felt her eyes blur with tears. She glanced at Ty. She was glad that she had trusted his opinion and decided to let Hannah ride Spartan. She could see from his face that he felt the same.

"Doesn't Spartan look happy?" he said softly.

Amy nodded.

Ty squeezed her shoulder. "Thank you for trusting me – about Hannah's riding, I mean."

"I always trust you," Amy said, surprised by the words that sprang to her lips.

"Just one more fence to go!" she heard Shelley Boswell say.

With a start, Amy turned her eyes back to the ring. With perfect timing, Spartan cleared the last jump and the audience burst into applause. Hannah circled him past the entrance and then patted him as if she was never going to stop and brought him back to a walk.

Amy, Ty and Shelley Boswell hurried to the collecting ring to meet her. "That was incredible!" Amy said.

"Well done!" Ty said, smiling at Hannah.

"He was perfect!" she said, jumping off. "Amy, thanks for the advice – I gave him a little nudge when he seemed nervous and he was fine." Hannah turned to Spartan and rubbed his face. "You were fabulous!"

Amy smiled. At that moment everything seemed really good. And then she saw Ashley and Val Grant walk past them, their faces set. They had obviously been watching. "I guess Ashley won't be so quick to put Spartan down any more," Amy said with a grin. She stroked the horse's nose and he pushed against her hand.

There was a nerve-racking wait for the results, and at last the loudspeaker crackled into action. "Results of the equitation over fences, fourteen- to seventeen-year-olds," a voice said.

Hannah looked nervously at Amy. "You know I don't even care if I place. It's enough to have had a great round."

Amy looked at Hannah as the announcer continued.

"In first place, number three-six-five — Hannah Boswell on Dancing Grass Geronimo."

"You did it, Hannah!" Amy cried. "You qualified for the state finals."

"Oh my goodness!" Hannah gasped in astonishment. She hugged her grandmother. "Grandma! Gerry's won!" Suddenly, Hannah was mounting Spartan. Mrs Boswell brushed over her riding boots. Amy hurried to check Spartan's girth.

"Go on. You're in!" Ty said, seeing the ringmaster waiting.

Grinning from ear to ear, Hannah rode into the ring.

It didn't take long for the ribbons to be given out. Ashley was in second place and she looked thunderous — not even nodding a thank you as she received her red ribbon.

At last it was time for Hannah to lead the lap of honour

around the ring. As Spartan cantered past, Amy felt Ty's hand on her shoulder.

"You know, that was a really nice thing to do," he said softly.

Amy met his eyes. "Thanks," she smiled.

"Thank you so much for letting me ride Gerry — I mean Spartan," Hannah said again a little while later, as she and Amy led Spartan back to the Heartland trailer. "He really is wonderful — you are going to take him in lots of shows yourself, aren't you?"

Amy's heart sank slightly. "Well, it depends when we find him a new home."

"You can't keep him?" Hannah said, sounding surprised.

Amy shook her head. "At Heartland it's our policy to try and re-home the horses that we heal."

Hannah looked sadly at the horse. "Poor Gerry. He seems happy with you."

"Not as happy as he could be," Amy sighed. She decided to confide in Hannah. "I feel as if there's this bit of his heart that's locked away," she said. "The only times I've seen him look truly happy were when your grandfather came and then just now, with you."

"If only Grandpa would have him back, or if only I could have him." Hannah looked upset. "It's not fair," she said.

Amy stared at her, an idea leaping into her mind. "Well, why can't you? You said you were looking for a horse. You want one that can jump – Spartan would be perfect!"

Hannah looked startled. "*Me* have *Gerry* ... Grandpa would never agree. He gets upset whenever Gerry's name is mentioned."

Amy's flicker of hope died. "Oh." She sighed.

"But then, maybe it could work!" Hannah said, her mind looking as if it was suddenly working overtime. "I can't tell Grandpa that I want Gerry, because he'll say no. But if I ring him and say that I've found a brilliant jumper at the show that I want to buy ... if I just turn up with him..."

Amy stared at her. "What would your grandpa say? Wouldn't he go crazy?"

Hannah shook her head. "I don't think he would. Despite what he says, he really misses Gerry and I'm sure he would never be able to turn him away." She grabbed Amy's arm, her eyes suddenly shining in excitement. "Amy! This could really work! Let me ask Grandma and see what she says."

It took Hannah only a few minutes to persuade her grandmother that her plan was a good one. Amy rang Lou on the mobile to tell her the news.

"So he's going now?" Lou said in astonishment.

"Yes," Amy said. "The Boswells' trailer isn't big enough but Ty has said that he'll drive Spartan and me there in our trailer."

"It's supposed to be Ty's day off!" Lou said. "Look, tell him to bring the trailer back here and I'll drive you and Spartan on to the Boswells'."

"OK," Amy said, switching the phone off and going to tell Ty.

Soon it was all arranged. Hannah and Shelley Boswell would go ahead with Sinbad and let Larry Boswell know about the "new" arrival.

"I'll get his old stall ready for him," Hannah said, giving Spartan a last pat before setting off with her grandma. "Now, you've got the directions?"

Amy nodded.

Hannah grinned at her. "Then I'll see you in a couple of hours."

Ty drove Amy and Spartan back to Heartland. "Well, I guess this is goodbye, fella," he said, going into the trailer as Lou got her things together. He patted Spartan. "Be happy."

"He will," Amy said softly, looking at Spartan's handsome bay head. She knew she was doing the right thing.

Lou came out of the house. "Are we ready, then?"

Amy nodded. "See you tomorrow, Ty — and thanks for everything."

"No problem," Ty said, smiling. He turned and strode off down the yard. Amy quickly got into the pick-up.

Lou opened the door and jumped in beside her. "Right, let's go!"

As the trailer bumped down the drive, Amy heard Spartan

whinny. A sharp memory of Spartan being in the back of the trailer and Mom, not Lou, sitting beside her leapt into Amy's mind. Then, Amy and Mom had been trying to save Spartan. She glanced at her sister – now she and Lou were trying to make him happy.

She swallowed as she thought about the last three months. She had lost so much and yet, looking at Lou now and remembering the decision her sister had made the night before, she suddenly realized that she had gained something, too.

Larry Boswell's stud farm was set deep in the rolling countryside to the south of Virginia. Amy looked out of the window as they drove past farm after farm. At last they reached Dancing Grass Stud. Dark wooden fences separated the paddocks from the road. A heavy wooden sign swung in the slight breeze.

"Looks like we're here," said Lou.

Amy felt a prickle of apprehension as they turned up the driveway. What if Hannah was wrong? What if Larry Boswell wouldn't accept Spartan and they had to take him home again?

Lou drove up to the front of the farmhouse and they got out and looked around. No one came to meet them. "I'll go and knock," Lou said. There was no reply from the front door, so she went round the back.

Amy went to check on Spartan. He gave a little nicker

when he saw her. Amy slowly walked up to him. His dark eyes looked at her calmly. She wondered what the future would hold for him. What would Larry Boswell decide?

Just then she heard the sound of voices approaching from the back of the trailer. "That's the Heartland trailer!" she heard Larry Boswell say. His tone turned angry. "What are *they* doing here?"

Amy froze and then she heard Hannah speak. "They're delivering the horse I rode at the show, Grandpa. The one I told you that I want."

Suddenly she heard Lou's voice. "Hi," her sister said, coming from the direction of the house. "We finally got here. Hello, Mr Boswell."

"Hi," Amy heard Larry Boswell say gruffly.

"So are you ready to see him, Grandpa?" Hannah asked eagerly.

"Amy's in there with him," Lou said.

Hannah suddenly appeared in the side door. "Amy, hi! Are you ready to bring him out?" She must have seen Amy's face because she smiled. "Don't worry," she said in a low voice. "It'll be fine. Trust me."

She disappeared and Amy heard the locks on the ramp being undone. She placed a hand on Spartan's bay neck and felt the warmth of his satin-smooth skin. *Is this finally goodbye?* she thought. After everything that had happened to them both, it seemed almost impossible to believe.

"Spartan, you're back at Dancing Grass Stud," Amy said.

"We've been through so much since the last time you were here." Amy put her cheek against his graceful head. "I'm going to miss you, boy, but I think this is where you belong."

Amy heard the ramp being lowered and she steadily led Spartan out.

Larry Boswell stared at Spartan incredulously. Before he could speak, Spartan nickered and pulled at the lead-rope. Amy let go of the halter and stood back. The horse trotted over to his beloved owner. Lifting his muzzle to Larry Boswell's face, he snorted and then buried his head in the man's shoulder.

"Gerry!" Larry Boswell said, reaching out and touching the horse's neck. Spartan pushed against his chest and nuzzled him, his nostrils flaring as he breathed in his owner's scent. "Oh, Gerry," Larry Boswell murmured.

"Grandpa, Gerry's the horse that I won on at the show," Hannah said softly. "You wouldn't believe it. He was amazing in the ring and he's the horse I want." She went up to her grandpa and took his hand. "Please say that I can keep him. Please say that you'll let Gerry stay."

Amy held her breath as Larry Boswell hesitated. Then suddenly a tear ran down his cheek. "Yes," he said, brushing it quickly away and looking at Hannah. "He can stay."

Soon Spartan was settled happily back in his old stall, as if the immense trauma of the last few months had never happened.

"We should be going," Lou said to Shelley Boswell. "I'm glad it all worked out so well in the end."

"Me too, honey," Shelley Boswell smiled.

Amy said goodbye to Hannah and then walked over to where Spartan was looking out of his stall. He turned his head towards her, his ears pricked, his silky forelock tumbling down over his handsome face. Love shone unmistakably in his eyes. Amy felt a lump of tears gather in her throat. At last, Spartan's heart was unlocked.

She put a hand on his neck. "I told you I would make you happy, Spartan," she whispered as he nuzzled her hair. "Well, I've kept my promise." Feeling the tears gather in her throat, she shut her eyes tightly and kissed his face, knowing that it would be for the last time.

Swallowing painfully, she turned and walked over to the pick-up where Lou was waiting.

"I'll write!" Hannah called. "And send you photos."

As Amy opened the door and got in, she saw Larry Boswell walking over to Spartan's stall. Spartan whinnied softly and Amy saw Larry Boswell's face crease into a delighted smile.

Suddenly she felt Lou squeeze her shoulder. "You did the right thing, Amy," she said. "Everyone needs a home and you know that Heartland could never really have been Spartan's."

Amy looked at her sister. "But it is yours now, isn't it, Lou?"

Lou smiled. "Yes," she replied. "It is." Her eyes met Amy's and she started the engine. "Come on," she said softly. "Let's go home."

Read More about

Healing horses, healing hearts...

LAUREN BROOKE

HEARTLAND

Coming Home

Healing horses, healing hearts. . .

LAUREN BROOKE

HEARTLAND

Breaking Free

Healing horses, healing hearts. . .

LAUREN BROOKE

HEARTLAND

Taking Chances

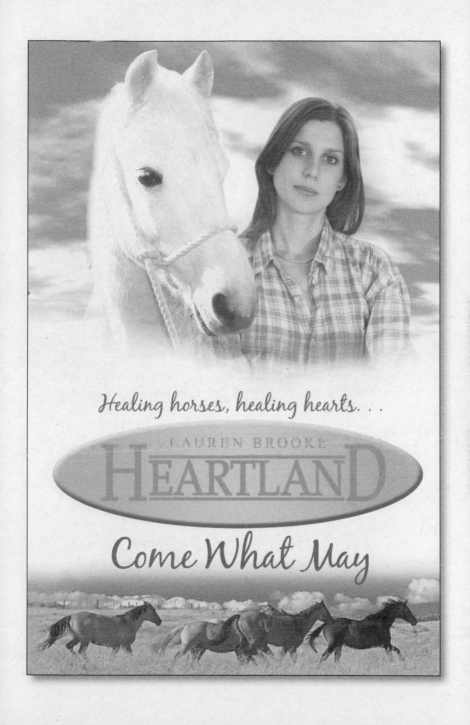

Healing horses, healing hearts. . .

LAUREN BROOKE

HEARTLAND

Come What May

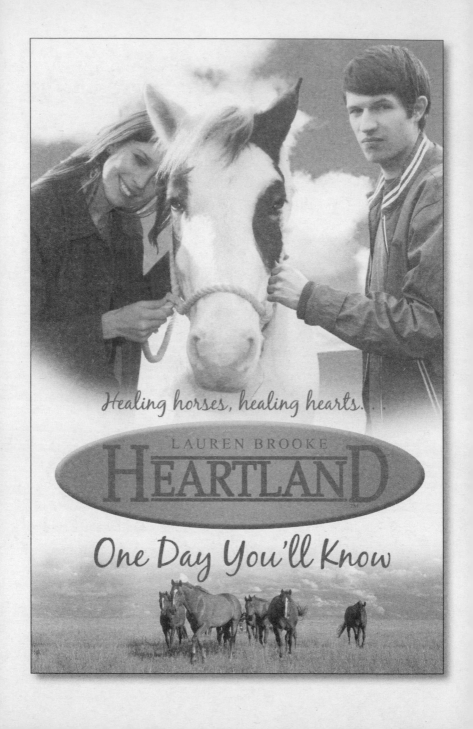

Healing horses, healing hearts...

LAUREN BROOKE

HEARTLAND

One Day You'll Know

Scholastic Children's Books would like to thank
Vauxhall City Farm for their support and co-operation in
the production of this book. We couldn't have done it
without them or their horses.

Vauxhall City Farm is a charity providing a number of
projects including Riding for the Disabled lessons and
subsidised riding lessons for local inner city children.

History:

Vauxhall City Farm started out in 1977 with local people working voluntarily to transform derelict land into an oasis of country life in the heart of London. The farm attracts people from all around the UK to visit animals that live so near to Big Ben and who are at home in the hustle and bustle of inner London.

On the Farm

The Farm is a sensory experience with smells to accompany the bleating, mooing, neighing and oinking.

A walk through the farm takes you pass the goats and cows, with the help of signs and our committed volunteers, we try to make everyone's experience of the animals as positive and interactive as possible. If you carry on through the farm you reach the duck pond and the community garden.

Just outside the farm you can watch the animals grazing in the paddocks or a riding lesson in the school. Down by the horse paddocks live the chickens and rabbits, with a lovely ecology green space in which to eat your picnic.

Riding centre

We have a horse riding centre which provides subsidised riding lessons for local children, along with Riding for the Disabled and private lessons.

School activities

The Farm provides tours for schools and nursery groups with themes such as animal care, healthy eating and growing.

Vauxhall City Farm has disabled access to all public areas; please call us to for further details and/or book lessons or visits.

Ways to support Vauxhall City Farm:

Donations

Entrance to the farm is free but we depend upon the generosity of all our supporters and we're very grateful to everyone who makes a donation.

Animal Sponsorship

You can sponsor any animal from a guinea pig to a horse for yourself or as a gift. We will send you a certificate.

Corporate Sponsorship

We have several companies who have sponsored the horses and our larger livestock. Our horses give disabled children the chance to experience the joys of riding.

Volunteering

We welcome skilled and non-skilled volunteers, the farm recognises the importance of sharing skills and knowledge. The farm is unique in its volunteering programme, bringing all ages together and creating value in social interaction.

For more information about any of the above please contact linda.hinds@btconnect.com or vcf@btconnect.com

Vauxhall City Farm,
165 Tyers Street,
London SE11 5HS
0207 582 4204

www.vauxhallcityfarm.org

If you liked Heartland, try this. . .

Chestnut Hill
The New Class

Lauren
Brooke

By the author of *Heartland*

SCHOLASTIC

If you liked Heartland, try this. . .

Chestnut Hill
Making Strides

Lauren Brooke

By the author of *Heartland*

Chestnut Hill

Heart of Gold

Lauren Brooke

By the author of *Heartland*

SCHOLASTIC

If you liked Heartland, try this. . .

If you liked Heartland, try this...

If you liked Heartland, try this. . .

Chestnut Hill
Team Spirit
Lauren Brooke

By the author of *Heartland*

SCHOLASTIC